THE WAY I DIE

ALSO BY DEREK HAAS

The Silver Bear

Columbus

Dark Men

The Right Hand

A Different Lie

THE WAY I DIE

DEREK HAAS

PEGASUS CRIME

NEW YORK LONDON

THE WAY I DIE

Pegasus Books, Ltd.
148 W 37th Street, 13th Floor
New York, NY 10018

First Pegasus Books edition April 2018

Interior design by Maria Fernandez

Library of Congress Cataloging-in-Publication Data is available.

ISBN: 978-1-68177-662-0

10 9 8 7 6 5 4 3 2 1

Printed in the United States of America
Distributed by W. W. Norton & Company

For Claiborne and Jessica,

who inspire

THE WAY I DIE

I

The way I die is two taps to the head, stuffed in the trunk of a rental sedan, my body set on fire. The way I die is both arms broken, both legs broken, tossed off a cigarette boat in the middle of Lake Michigan, bricks in my pockets to weigh down the corpse. The way I die is acid in a bathtub, pushed out of an airplane, strung up and gutted in an old textile warehouse in Boston.

My name is Copeland. My name is Columbus.

The way I die is a shotgun in my mouth, my finger on the trigger.

—⚉—

It is the middle of February on Mackinac Island, a tiny community off the northern Michigan coast that battens down like an old sailing frigate in the winter months. Even the Arnold Line Ferry stops running after December, and until an ice bridge forms between the island and St. Ignace, the residents are on their own. Most of the islanders live in Harrisonville, in the center of the island, about 500 residents total, and they gather to watch school basketball or take cooking classes or drink coffee at the General Store, finding comfort in community. I do not join them.

The way I die is a knife under the ribs, a knife in my belly, a knife across my throat.

My cottage is in British Landing, on the northern tip of the island, isolated from isolation. Everyone does not know everyone here as outsiders might think, and I have managed to keep to myself. I live monastically, with just enough warmth, enough food, enough light to survive. Humans have always sought out punishment, begged for it, prayed for it, welcomed it, as though suffering and absolution are conjoined twins. I deserve punishment but not forgiveness. For the darkness I brought to innocent people, God demands pain.

The way I die is exposure. The way I die is thirty feet from the back door of this island cottage, frozen to death, a coat, snow pants, boots within a stone's throw.

I have lived here for eight months. I have enough money to pay my rent and feed myself indefinitely. I have enough money to keep moving from forgotten patch to forgotten patch without need for explanation as to why I suddenly pull up stakes. I always pay in cash, with enough on top to keep landlords from filling out forms or asking personal questions.

I had a family; I have no family. I had a son; I have no son. I am Copeland. I am Columbus.

The way I die is forgotten and alone.

A board in the window frame of my kitchen overlooking the side yard broke loose in heavy winds last night. The pane clattered like a ghost rattling chains, and so this morning, I walk to the general store in Harrisonville. The distance is two miles in the cold, but the wind has stopped raging like so many things do in the light of day, and I leave my face uncovered. A woman waves from her yard as I go by, but it's cursory, and she's already spun with her paper and returned inside her front door without waiting to see if I return the gesture.

The store is thinly populated with residents clustered near the register, steam from their coffee cups warming their faces as they take turns on the day's events, the weather, politics. Four men and a woman, they nod at me as I enter. I nod back and am grateful that that's all they need to satisfy the social contract. Maybe I can live on this island longer than I thought.

I find an aisle filled with hardware and grab assorted boxes of nails, a hammer, a wood planer, a sander. A man named Aiza threatened me with these same tools in the basement of a toy shop in Madrid. That was before he was beheaded, his body stuffed into the trunk of a rental car. Tools made to repair things should be used for their intended purposes.

A girl in her midteens, short, fat, wearing glasses, moves into my peripheral vision and looms. I turn to face her and she doesn't lower her gaze, just keeps staring at me with cow's eyes.

"I can find what I'm looking for, thanks," I say.

She chews on a piece of beef jerky, her jaw working horizontally. "Oh, I don't work here. My mom's just getting some coffee."

I turn back to the shelves and look over the sandpaper, hoping she'll get the message. She doesn't take the hint.

"What's your name?"

I blow out an exaggerated breath, slowly turn back. "Jack."

"Meghan. Nice to meet you."

I grab the first packet of sandpaper I can find, toss it into my hand basket, and step past her toward the register. I check out, pay in cash, shoulder my bag of tools like I'm Santa Claus on Christmas Eve, and head for the door. Meghan stays where I left her, chewing sloppily on her jerky, watching me the whole way.

The way I die is a rope slung over a barn beam, a chair overturned underneath my jerking feet.

I've got the new wood shaped, planed, and in place when I see her moving up the driveway in the reflection from the windowpane. *You've got to be kidding me.* Did she follow me the two miles back here? If so, what does that say about my diminishing skills that I didn't see her?

"Hey, Jack," she offers. "Meghan. From the store. You fixing a window?"

"I am, yeah." I put every effort into my body language to tell her I'd rather be left alone, but she's incapable of getting the message. She toes the snow on my driveway. Her cheeks are red above a knit scarf.

"There's a teacher at my school. Mr. Laughlin? He lets the kids come over to his house and watch movies."

I don't answer.

"He's never said it's okay for me to come. He's never *not* said it, but he's never said it."

I get out a nail and pound it into place.

"I live up the street. I saw you move in."

4

A second nail goes in. She waits for me to stop pounding the hammer, and as soon as I do, she fills the silence.

"I talk to the horses sometimes. I don't have my own, but the Prescotts let me go in their barn. They've got one named Star and one named Sammy. They're good listeners. The horses, not the Prescotts."

I turn to face her. "Meghan? Listen to me. I don't like talking. I don't like listening. I don't like people, okay?"

"That's just sad," she says with no judgment in her voice. She doesn't move.

I turn back to the window frame, but her reflection stays right where it is. I pound a third nail into the opposite corner, watch until the head embeds in the wood.

"People don't think you can get lonely here, but you can," she says.

I position a fourth nail.

"I'll come back when you feel like talking."

When the nail's head hits the wood, I look in the reflection and she's gone.

Inside, I fish a beer out of the refrigerator and drain it with my back to the sink in the kitchen. There's a card on my otherwise empty counter. It came in the mail three days ago. It reads, "Call me."

I won't, but I haven't thrown it away.

—⁓—

Mr. Laughlin's first name is Spencer and he lives alone in a big house on a hill near Four Corners. His parents owned the house before him and his grandparents before that. He teaches English and History at the combination junior high and high school, and he stays late to lead an extracurricular poetry class for a half dozen girls. A few weekend nights a month, he invites a few of the girls up to his house on the hill to watch Netflix. He provides blankets and popcorn and sneaks the girls some beer if they promise not to tell their parents. Meghan, indeed, is not invited.

I learn all this from standing in the snow, from looking through windows, from making myself invisible the way I have on countless assignments. I've seen Mr. Laughlin's behavior before, a predator's view of the world, and whether or not Mr. Laughlin is building to a crescendo or this is just the eye of a hurricane, I have no idea. What I do know is he's going to abuse these children who trust him. He's a wolf, waiting for one weak member of the flock to separate herself. What he doesn't know is there are animals bigger than wolves in the woods.

I walk back toward my house, the temperature biting wherever it can find a millimeter gap in my winter gear. What am I doing? I don't care about these people. I don't care about myself. I don't care about anyone anymore. I'm a plane with a loss of cabin pressure, an unconscious pilot, drifting across America, unsure where to crash.

Meghan waits for me on my driveway. She holds up a hand as I approach as if I can't see her there from a mile away. "You look cold," she says.

"Meghan."

"How's your window?"

"Fixed."

"You go get some coffee?"

I look back over my shoulder, the direction from which I came. "Yeah."

"No, you didn't," she says, wiping her nose with a mitten. "You came from Mr. Laughlin's house where you were peeking in the window."

I keep the surprise off my face, just narrow my eyes. Meghan's expression is guileless. "That's Laura, Kim, Tiffany, Beth, and Gretchen who go over there."

I don't respond. Meghan sniffs, wipes her nose again with her other hand, then pushes up her glasses. "Why were you looking in his window?"

"Why were you following me?"

She shrugs her shoulders as if that's an acceptable answer. "Gretchen thinks her poetry is something special, because Mr. Laughlin tells her it is. He tells her she could get published. No way. I read it. It sucks. No way."

"Meghan, I'm cold, I'm hungry, and I'm tired. I'm going inside now. Don't follow me again."

"Fine," she says. She starts to move past me, wobbling side to side in her parka as she moves forward, like that much bulk is just too cumbersome to move in one direction. *"The snow covers the ground like a blanket, and I close my eyes tight.* That's her poetry. It's shit. You know it. I know it," Meghan fumes and marches away.

I move up the steps, turn my key in the lock, and enter my house.

The way I die is from indifference.

There was a time when I would have puzzled over who posed more of a threat to me, the solicitous poetry teacher who has no knowledge I exist or the bovine fifteen-year-old who is following me around the island. There was a time when I would've known a not particularly artful teen was trailing me long before she told me, but that time has passed.

I'm a dull blade, a triggerless gun.

I'm a sleepwalker.

I'm drifting with the current, an oarless canoe spinning in an eddy.

An idea cements in my mind, hardening in a mold. If I eliminate the teacher, I'll have to move on. Maybe this is as it should be. Take out a few evil people on my way off the planet and balance my ledger with a small measure of good.

I have skills that are dormant, rusty, but not forgotten.

I can start here on this island, kill this high school teacher before he ruins the lives of guiltless girls, and disappear to a new town until I find someone else who deserves to have his ticket punched.

The way I die is righteousness.

—w—

I wake early and go through a routine to activate abeyant muscles— sit-ups, push-ups, chin-ups. I'm alert before the sun arrives, before Meghan comes looking for me, up and out and moving as a morning dusting of snow descends from a gray sky, fat and heavy enough to cover my tracks.

The high school door has a simple lock, and before I go to work on it, I try the latch and it gives. No one seems to be worried about vandalism or theft.

The school is a series of brick structures with a few classrooms, a library, a gym with the name Mackinac Island Lakers painted in cursive along one wall, and what looks like an all-purpose room, more of a rec center than a traditional bastion of education. The place is as silent as a graveyard, and I'm starting to feel better than I have in the last two years. I'm in a location I'm not supposed to be, I'm setting a trap for prey that has no idea I'm coming, and I'm already thinking in old, comfortable patterns, seeing kill spots and escape routes.

Am I supposed to be here? Not killing for money, not serving a master, but transforming into judge, jury, and executioner based on *my* code, *my* morals?

A door clicks open, the same door I entered, and I slip into a classroom, smooth as glass, expending just enough energy to propel my feet forward while I keep my body still. There is a way of moving from room to room when avoiding threats that draws little attention. The instinct to flee causes reactions at a speed that counters intentions. Big movements are what attract eyeballs. Heavy footsteps sound in the room, but that's not uncommon in this heavy snow, so I can't tell if it's a man or woman who entered. I reposition myself so I can use the reflection of a mirror off of a window to catch a glimpse of my co-intruder, and my heart beats faster. It's Mr. Laughlin, all by himself, hours before the school bell.

It rings for thee, Mr. Laughlin, I think, and realize this might be the first time I've thought of something funny since Risina died and I gave my son away to a safe family. There is the grieving that is endless because the way you grieve is the whole of your life, the sixty minutes, the twenty-four hours of each day. It's the shut-in, the can't-get-out-of-bed, the curtains drawn. It's the cemetery visitor. It's the I-can't-bear-to-clean-out-his-room. It's the lonely island on the fringes of the map. It's the cold without a jacket. It's the pain without a salve.

Then there are the ones who work themselves out of grief, who lose themselves in a higher purpose, in something bigger than individual suffering.

The way I die is to kill.

I watch Mr. Laughlin stamp his feet near the door to knock the snow off his boots. He finds a hook for his coat and flips on some electric lights so the all-purpose room is lit in a bluish glow, energy-saving bulbs that don't quite cut through darkness as well as their predecessors.

He trundles to a cluster of beanbag chairs, moves a couple of them to form a lopsided circle, then satisfied, he heads to a desk in the corner, whistling a tuneless melody. He behaves like a man who is comfortable, safe in his domain. He is incautious, unobservant.

He reaches into a desk drawer and removes a journal, takes out a pen, and taps it against his lower lip as he reads. What he's writing in this notebook, at this hour, I have no idea, but I think I might want to have a look at it when this is over. Maybe take it with me when I leave this island and read it when I've put some distance between his body and mine.

From my vantage point, I search around the room for a weapon that will get the job done, and my eyes fall on a row of plastic bins, one marked *crayons*, a second *colored pencils*, a third *glue*, and the fourth *scissors*. Without a sound, I cross to the bins and find what I'm looking for, a large set of teacher's scissors, the grips reinforced and the tip sharp as a knife. I return to my vantage point, and Mr. Laughlin is where I left him, tapping that pen against his lip and every now and then jotting down a word or a phrase or a sentence. He's absorbed in his work, and he'll never hear me coming.

My pulse slows. I'm an athlete who stands at the plate for the first time in years, a pitch hurtling toward him at ninety miles an hour, and my body takes over as muscles twitch and respond and jerk to life. Fifty feet across low light separates the back of Mr. Laughlin's neck from this pair of scissors.

He drops the journal from the desk to his lap and swivels his chair away from me, so he's facing the wall, oblivious, and the world is telling me this is right, this is good, this is the higher purpose, this is what you're meant to do, take him now.

I am Columbus.

As I am about to emerge from my hiding spot, the front door *clunk-clunks* open and a fifteen-year-old girl enters. Mr. Laughlin smiles, a fat spider on a web. The girl sheds her coat, and underneath, she's wearing jeans that look like they were painted on, and a tight sweater stretched to the breaking point. I haven't seen her before, but I've seen her before. I've seen her in red light districts in Barcelona, in Paris, in

Prague, in Vegas. She has the wide-eyed innocent face of a little girl and the much-too-adult body of a grown woman, hair and makeup and clothes chosen to emphasize the latter when she should be doing all she can to hold on to the former.

"Gretchen," Mr. Laughlin says, and the way he says it, he's expecting her.

"Mr. Laughlin," she calls back, already a tickle in her voice.

"Come here, come here," he calls. "Sit, sit," but she moves to the beanbag circle and plops down on the first one, smiling as she does. Her backpack drops next to her and she unzips it and pulls out a folder.

"Why are you making me come in so early?" she calls out and looks up at the clock.

Mr. Laughlin finishes writing whatever will be his last recorded words, tucks the notebook in his desk drawer, and stands. "I'm not making you do anything, Gretchen. I *offered* to take a look at your essay and *offered* to meet you on *my* time. You chose to accept my offer."

"Whatever," Gretchen says, the universal word for a teenager's unsuccessful attempt at indifference.

He crosses the room slowly, a ballet he wants to extend, a symphony he wants to drive to climax, then drops into the beanbag chair opposite her. She pulls at her hair absently, a nervous tic, then sticks the tips into the corner of her mouth.

"Show it to me. The essay . . ." he offers, and my grip tightens on the scissors' handle. He's toying with her, he's a shark circling, a monster in the closet, and I despise him, a feeling as familiar to me as an old friend.

The way I die is to hate.

She withdraws a journal from her backpack like the one he had at his desk and hands it to him. As he takes it, she holds on to her end, so they're both touching it at the same time and poor Gretchen is playing with fire and is too dumb to realize it. She lets go, and

11

Mr. Laughlin chuckles like rain beating on a tin roof. He clucks his tongue in an exaggerated *tsk, tsk*, and it's all I can do to keep from sprinting across the room and burying these scissors handle deep into the base of his neck, splattering his gore all over her face, but that would be it for me and for some reason I can't explain, my innate sense of self-preservation remains healthy. I'm going to kill him this morning, but I'm going to get away with it without any witnesses.

Mr. Laughlin leans back and reads Gretchen's essay while she fiddles with her hair. "Umm-hmmm," he hums every now and then, or adds an "okay, okay," or "that's interesting" while she sits on the beanbag chair, a baby bird waiting on worms. After an interminable ten minutes, he snaps the journal shut so that it makes her jump, and he starts laughing.

"It's very good, Gretchen. Very good," he purrs, and her face brightens. It's that easy. A little flattery. A little making her wait for it, making her *beg* for it, and he has her, the predator, the bastard. "When you wrote of the gathering storm, what was the allegory you were trying to convey?"

"Oh, I don't know. I was just like trying to, you know, say that like my family is sometimes, you know, sort of fighting like a storm."

"Uh-huh, uh-huh," he says as she explains, and the prick isn't even using *allegory* correctly and I'm going to shove his faux intellect straight down his throat.

He stands and closes on her, choosing at the last moment to fall on top of the beanbag chair next to hers. She stops playing with her hair and shifts closer to him, pulling her sweater tighter across her chest, hoping he'll notice, and she's rewarded with a widening of his eyes. He's not done playing though, savoring every moment, a meal made sweeter by forcing himself to wait.

He opens her notebook again and points to something so she'll have to lean closer still. "You use the word *lightening* here."

"Yes. Like lightening, in a storm," she responds.

"Oh . . ." he pretends to suddenly be enlightened by this revelation, as though it isn't a common mistake and he never would have guessed that lightning is what she meant. "Oh, you see, you spelled it with an *e*, which means 'lightening,' like when the sun comes up and there is more light in the sky."

For a moment, she has no idea what he's talking about, and then understanding hits her with the subtlety of a sledgehammer. Gretchen smiles broadly and her mouth shows a row of uneven teeth. He beams back at her with a bit of flirt in his voice that is as stomach-churning as a bucket of vomit, and says, "There's no *e* in the 'lightning' you mean," and he leans in close to her so their foreheads are almost touching, and I don't care if she is a witness, I am going to kill this man right here, right now, in front of her, but before I step into the room, a loud BANG reverberates through the school as the front door flies open and smacks into the neighboring wall like a cymbal crashing.

Mr. Laughlin's neck snaps up to see what intrusion ruined his triumphant moment, and his eyes narrow when he sees it is Meghan. My old friend Meghan, who looks around like it's the most natural thing in the world for her to be at school an hour and a half before the first class. She does a theatrical shake, says "Brrrrr," takes off her coat, turns like she's surprised someone else is here, and shouts, "Gretchen! Mr. Laughlin! This is a surprise."

Good ol' Meghan, employing the oldest trick in the book for children dealing with adults: underestimation.

Mr. Laughlin stands quickly, like a dog over a spilled flowerpot, and stammers, "Meghan, I . . . we were . . . Gretchen and I were having a private study session."

Meghan strolls over to the beanbag circle and drops into the one next to Gretchen, the one Mr. Laughlin vacated.

"It's a *private* lesson," Gretchen spits petulantly at Meghan. She might've stuck out her tongue had she been a few years younger. Instead, she does so with her chin.

"Oh, is it private? Like tutoring? My mom says I need tutoring but I don't . . . I just don't always feel like doing homework so I don't want one."

Mr. Laughlin looks at Meghan, sorting choices. How can he get rid of her? How can he do it without Meghan figuring out his true purpose?

Before he can say anything, Meghan interrupts those thoughts. "Mr. Laughlin, if I told my mom you give private tutoring in the early morning hours like you do with Gretchen all alone, do you think she'd let me take private lessons too?"

I can't see her mouth from my vantage point, but I know she has a smile working. Not much, just a hint, so that Mr. Laughlin knows she knows, knows he's stuck.

He looks down at his shirt and tries to smooth the wrinkles with fussy fingers. "Uh, Meghan, why don't we discuss this later? I'll speak to your mother and we can—"

"It's just that I get confused sometimes . . . like what's the difference between *lightening* with an *e* and *lightning* without the *e*, you know? Maybe that's the kind of thing you could help me with . . . in your private lessons, I mean."

Now both Gretchen and Mr. Laughlin look at her with new understanding. She has been watching them longer than they thought. Before they have a chance to voice a word, she interrupts again. "Anyway," and she digs through her backpack, "you guys don't mind me. I have to finish my math before the bell rings so I'm just gonna do it right here while you guys continue your private lesson. I will be as quiet as a mouse and you won't even know I'm here."

She shuffles through papers as Mr. Laughlin sniffs, then turns and walks toward his desk, defeated.

"Oh, were you finished?" Meghan calls out. "I didn't mean to interrupt right when you were getting good into your private lesson."

Gretchen rises to her feet in a huff, turning red, and bolts to the bathroom. Mr. Laughlin pulls his journal from his desk drawer and writes quietly.

From her spot on top of the beanbag chair, Meghan chuckles, and right before I back away from my hiding spot, I can't be sure, but I think she looks in my direction.

—⚋—

I pick my way through the snow as the sun rises and sparkles the diamonds of the snowdrifts. Meghan's gonna knock down some walls in her day if she makes it off this island. She's a bulldozer, a wrecking ball. She has the disposition of some of the greatest killers I know—razor-sharp wit buried inside a forgettable package. Hmmm . . . maybe I'll come back here someday, years from now, when Mr. Laughlin's murder is a different generation's folklore. Maybe I'll come back and check on Meghan. Maybe I'll catch up to her right when she's about to mark a new chapter in her life and suggest a path she can take that's not so common.

I warm as I hike the miles back to my house on the edge of the island. I'm not sure how I'm going to kill the schoolteacher, but I know I'll do it in the next twenty-four hours, before he has a chance to give another private lesson, one without Meghan there to interrupt.

I turn the key to my front door, crank the knob, step into my foyer, and remove my coat.

"This is some shit," Archibald Grant says as he walks out of my kitchen, into the light from the window, blowing on a cup of coffee.

The way I die is at the hands of a friend.

2

Archie is my fence, or was, before I quit killing privately and took up killing for the government. The change of employer cost me my wife, my son, my life, my sanity, my peace. It wasn't Archie's fault; he was a pawn like me, pieces moved around a chess-board until the king falls. For us, the board was picked up, slammed against the wall, tossed in the fire. When it ended, it ended ugly, and no one from that particular branch of dark men survived to claim us. Shaken, devastated, I handed my young son over to an old friend and set forward to end my life. I didn't want anyone to try to reach me through my son, so the best way to make that gulf inaccessible was to kill myself. It made sense, it was logical, it was smart, it was deserved. I planned to do it, I still do, but I want to suffer first. It seems righteous, somehow, to pass through the lake of fire before arriving in Hell.

So I called Archie and told him my plans, and he said he understood and faked my death to buy me time to do it right. The way I die is shot through the head by a rifle, a long-range sniper with a gossipy mouth told where and when to hit me, while I sit idle in the front seat of a BMW on the rooftop of a parking garage. The way I die is the shooter disintegrates my head, or what he thinks is my head, or what he is told is my head, even if it is a corpse placed there by Archie the night before. The shooter, a midlevel assassin named Crane, blabs to everyone between the Atlantic and Pacific that he has bagged Columbus, and Archie fans the flames just enough to turn the rumors into a brush fire. The name Columbus fades from rogues' lips. No one wants to romanticize a dead hit man who went out like a lamb.

From there, I build a wall between Columbus and Copeland, between my son, Pooley, and me, between the killer who stalked prey and the broken soul trudging around Mackinac Island. A stopgap, okay. A thumb in the dike until I deem my suffering enough to merit death. The devil promises torment, and if darkness is the end, I want damnation first.

I wander and I grieve and I take pain as comfort and I pick up and move and keep to myself and hurt privately and travel north, always north, until the landscape is cold and barren.

Here, Archie finds me.

Archibald "Archie" Grant is a tall, thin, black man who has survived a long time in the killing game by keeping his clients happy and his stable of assassins formidable. A fence in our business stands between the client and the killer so never the twain shall meet. The fence does the pre-assignment legwork and puts a file together on the target in order to give his contract killer several options to make a successful hit. Success doesn't just mean a dead target. It means getting away with it, too, so the murder ends in unsolved case files and inconclusive evidence. Archie may look like a refugee from a '70s-era pornography set, with his tan suits and matching shirts, his wide-brim fedoras, dangling cigarettes, and half smiles, but he is the best at what he does, and he's the only man on earth I trust, even if I dole out that trust reluctantly.

He takes a sip of his coffee and leans back in a chair so the front legs come off the floor. "Why didn't you get back to me?"

I shrug. "I was thinking about it."

"I send you a message that says 'Call me,' you pick up the phone. And don't say you didn't get it, 'cause I see it right over there." He nods at the counter, one eyebrow cocked.

"What do you want me to say? I was busy."

"Doing what? This place is the goddamn tundra."

"Nothing."

"Punishing yourself?"

I don't answer.

"Shit. You a mess." Archie studies me out of the tops of his eyes, that one eyebrow still arched.

I'm good at holding a poker face but I'm out of practice so my eyes flash. "No. Zero chance."

"Now hear me out. Hear me out before you go all wild-eyed. What do I call you now by the way?"

"Copeland."

"Okay, Cope. I like that. Hear me out, Cope. This ain't a job, not exactly. Not like you're used to. But it came to me in a pretty package with a bow on top, and I thought to myself, *I got the perfect man for it. He may not know it, he may not agree, but he's the perfect man for it.*" He points a finger gun at me and mimes pulling the trigger. "That's you, Mary Lou."

"Peggy Sue."

"What?"

"That's the expression. That's you, Peggy Sue."

"Expression? What the fuck are you . . . never mind. Don't correct my expressions. I'll use whatever expression I feel like."

I hang my head like the effort of even listening to Archie is too much for me. He keeps on harping on expressions so I get up and move to the refrigerator, surprised by how empty it is. "Next thing I know you're gonna be correcting my grammar and then we gonna have a prob—"

"What is it? The job. What is it?"

Archie sets all four legs of his chair on the floor and leans forward. "Like I say, you the perfect man for it. There's this cat in Portland who's got a price on his head. A big-ticket price that supposedly comes from Europe or Russia or some shit I'm not too sure about yet. He works in tech or a branch of tech or some kind of tech and crossed horns with the wrong kind of bull, and now he got a contract out on him. I'mma do the work but I'm not there yet. This just came to me, like I told you."

I return to the table with a pear from the fridge and a knife, start to chip off slices. "You want me to kill a nerd."

"I want you to let me finish."

He waits to see if I'll challenge him, but I eat my pear. "Anyway, this cat's about thirty days from getting his grave dug, only he gets tipped off it's coming. I'm not sure how, but that's the way it's told to me. We got a mutual acquaintance who works the periphery of what we do and this acquaintance reaches out to me. 'What can I do about this?' he asks me. Can his friend pay off this hit and make it go away? Will I find out where it's coming from because apparently this nerd's got some enemies. You play in the Eastern European sandbox, you gonna get bullies kicking sand in your face, no doubt. Running and hiding ain't an option for this guy, so I'm told. He has a business to run. Raising the white flag ain't an option either . . . you know as well as I do that's how you end up in the ground. 'So what can we do?' the acquaintance asks me. I tell him 'What your boy needs is *protection*. Someone who can see all the angles so when this assassin comes at him, this assassin walks into an ambush. Not bodyguards, no sir. Even the best bodyguards, you gonna get what you gonna get.' 'Oh, he's got bodyguards,' Curtis tells me. That's the mutual acquaintance, Curtis. Curtis says, 'Okay, okay, so what you thinking, Archie?' and I say, 'I'm thinking fight fire with fire. Your boy needs a hit man of his own. Someone who has taken out men. Someone who has done it a hundred times. Someone who knows the way this hit is going to go down, so he can stop it *from* going down. You need a Silver Bear,' and I'm thinking but I don't say, *You need Columbus*."

I cut off another slice of pear and offer it to Archie, but he holds up a hand to decline. "So whatchoo think?"

I take a bite of the fruit and the juice overwhelms my mouth. It tastes sour, not yet ripe. "I'm a killer."

"You *were*. Before all this," he interrupts, gesturing around the room. "I'm offering you a chance to be a *protector*. Which from where I'm sitting might be exactly what you need."

"What if the nerd deserves it?"

"He probably does, Cope. He probably does. And you can make that decision. I don't give a fuck. You wanna pull the matador's cape and let the bull come stick him, be my guest. I'll leave that up to you.

But I figure, look here, this is a chance to give you a fresh start, to dust off your skills, to wipe your slate clean, to stop wallowing in your self-pity. What you're doing is unseemly. And maybe . . . maybe Cope, maybe you can find a reason to live again, 'cause this ain't you." He shakes a cigarette from a pack of Camels and lights it up, takes a drag, then points the tip at me. "Plus, this nerd is rich as a motherfucker and willing to write a blank check, so maybe I kill two birds, you know what I'm saying?" He leans back like he doesn't need to tell me any more, takes a long drag, and lets the smoke out slowly so it gathers in the corner of the ceiling.

I exhale, turning it over in my mind. There are a million reasons to say no, but I can't think of one right now.

"When?" I ask.

"The clock's ticking. Shit, nerd might already be dead and this all be moot. But I tell you, he's *gonna* be dead if you don't help him. I know *that*. Either way, it's nothing to me. I'm just trying to help out Curtis and maybe help you out, too."

"Two birds?"

Archie grins, "That's it."

"You say he already has bodyguards."

"That's what Curtis tells me. I know nothing about them. I heard this story and come straight to you."

"Why's the nerd going to trust me?"

"Shiiiiit. He's not. It'll be up to my man to arrange things. You get him to trust you, or he don't, and it's over quick. What do you care?"

Archie knows he has me hooked and just has to reel in the line now. He stands and claps his hands together. "Let's get outta this dump. Get back to civilization, Columbus." He sniffs, but doesn't wipe his nose. "I mean Copeland. Won't make that mistake again." He holds his hands up, innocently.

I gather my coat and look around. My eyes fall on the window frame I fixed, the nails I hammered, the glass pane secured. It's holding.

Archie reads my thoughts like a good fence should. "I'll take care of everything."

"How'd you get here anyway?"

"Follow me, and I'll show you."

—⁂—

The prop plane takes to the sky with a bone-shuddering jolt. I look down at the little island, blanketed with fresh powder. It's easy to pick out the school: a couple of pitched rooftops in the center of the island. Classes just began, and I imagine Meghan in the front row, a tormenting eye on Mr. Laughlin.

"What?" Archie says, looking over at me in the two-seater behind the pilot.

—⁂—

In Chicago, Archie booked me into the Peninsula, and I shower, eat, and wait for him to call. A burner phone rests on the bedside table, and I climb under the covers and endure its silence. Darkness comes for me, and with it, inside it, are Risina's smile, Risina's kiss, Risina's touch, Risina's scent. For the first year, I ran from these images, but the darkness was a fire I couldn't outpace. I'd climb from bed, take a scalding shower, do push-ups, go for a walk, chop wood, anything to keep from burning in that fire. I could keep the flames at bay for a day or two, but then I'd close my eyes, exhausted, and she'd return, the woman I brought into this life, carelessly, recklessly, foolishly. She would smile, kiss, touch, and the fire would overwhelm me, punish me, suffocate me. I couldn't run, so I took the heat, wore it like a cloak, wrapped myself in it, until the pain wrecked me.

The phone rings. I'm not sure how long I've been in this hotel room, hours or days.

"Copeland," Archie's voice cuts through the fog. "Come on over. Curtis is here and he wants to talk at you."

"On my way," I answer, and hit the "end" button.

It takes a few minutes until I can push out of the fire and rise from bed.

Risina, I'm sorry. I didn't deserve your trust and I didn't deserve your love but the endless pain I suffer . . . I try to take on as much as I can so somehow, some way, maybe it can relieve some of *your* suffering. Perhaps the pain and terror and incomprehension you felt in those last few days can be reduced by my pain until the end of my days.

Can you save a past soul through present suffering?

Can you cleanse a dead loved one by consuming yourself in fire?

Aren't past, present, and future linked in the mind, in memory, in imagination? And if so, doesn't it make sense I can still save her?

I'll try, Risina.

Forever, I'll try.

Archie has an office in Mag Mile that enters off Ohio. There are no signs, no names on a pegboard letting you know what floor to exit the elevator. Three large men in suits greet you in the lobby and frisk you carefully before sending you through metal detectors. On the other side, two security cards must be waved in front of a scanner to send a visitor to the top floor. There, a wiry Nigerian man leads you to a waiting room where you are frisked and wanded again. Archie may look like he plays fast and loose, but he's a meticulously cautious fence. He's lived a long time working as a middleman in a business that exploits weaknesses, and he's done it through vigilance, cautiousness, and uncompromising professionalism. He wasn't always this skillful, but in the time since I joined him, he's watched and learned and grown. Other fences we've crossed paths with fall by the wayside as they accumulate mistakes. Archie does not plan to join them.

I'm shown into a large office with windows overlooking Millennium Park. From my vantage point, I see the Geary stage, the big bean, the video towers with the moving faces that soak kids in the summertime. Only a few bundled tourists brave the temperatures now, taking selfies with the sculptures.

I stand at the window, and if I shift my focus, I can see my reflection in the glass. I give myself a quick once-over, like a mechanic checking under the hood, and I have to say, I don't look so bad. I'm five foot eleven with skin the color of creamed coffee. My father was a white politician from New York and my mother was a black prostitute from outside of Baltimore, so my color is a match for my general disposition: a swirl of light and darkness. I'm thinner than usual by a solid ten pounds, the product of not caring about my appetite. I've lost some muscle too, but I can get that back. I don't look at my face often. There is nothing special about it, which is why I've had so much success as a contract killer. I never stand out in a crowd. I'm the invisible man Ralph Ellison wrote about, and I've practiced ways to make sure I'm forgotten by anyone who comes across me in the wild. No tattoos, no wild hair, nothing to stand out, nothing to get pointed to in a police book.

The door opens and Archie steps inside with a tall, dark-skinned black man wearing khakis and a sweater. "Copeland, this is Curtis, I was telling you about him. Curtis, Cope."

I nod a greeting and Archie gestures to a quartet of leather chairs facing a coffee table. I sit on one side, and Archie and Curtis the other.

"Copeland is a Silver Bear assassin," Archie begins. "That's a term the Russians use. Means he never defaults on a job, he'll take any assignment no matter how difficult, and he gets paid the high end of the high end."

Curtis assesses me but keeps his face inscrutable. "I know what it means. How come I never heard of him?"

"'Cause I wanted it that way," Archie answers. "You get a hitter like Cope, here, you break him too soon, you let his name build out there, you stir up hornets that don't need stirring up, you know what I'm saying?"

Curtis looks somewhere between satisfied and unsure.

Archie presses forward. He has an uncanny ability to take a non-answer for yes. "Tell us about this cat needs protecting."

Curtis measures me, then leans back like he's already dipped a toe in the pool just by being here, so he might as well sink to the bottom. "The man's name is Matthew Boone and he lives just outside of Portland, Oregon. He made a hundred million dollars writing code for facial recognition software, which got him connected to Homeland Security, which got him connected to the U.S. government, which got him connected to some Eastern Bloc countries, which got him a price on his head. He's not sure who, when, where, or how, but someone wants him dead, and he doesn't trust our government or foreign governments or nobody. He got a peek behind the curtain of the way the world *really* works, and it scared the hell out of him. That's the majority of what I know. He's scared and he doesn't wanna be dead."

I rise and pace, thinking it over. "How do you know him?"

Curtis rubs his hands. "We went to school together."

"Where?"

"MIT. He reached out because he heard what I do now."

"What do you do now, Curtis?"

"I make guns."

Curtis is full of surprises. He unfolds his hands like he's laying his history out on the table. "Handguns, rifles, assault rifles, semiautomatic rifles. Custom made."

"Legally?"

"Some. Enough. What do you carry?"

"Glock."

"Good weapon," Curtis nods. "There are advantages to a custom-made piece, you should know."

"I can imagine."

"I can hook you up."

"Maybe someday."

Curtis scratches an eyebrow with his thumb, looks at Archie, continues. "Anyway, Matthew Boone got spooked and reached out to me and I said I know a guy and maybe he can help."

"What kind of protection detail does he have in place?"

Curtis anticipates my question. "Two teams, twenty-four hours, seventy-two on, seventy-two off. I can't vouch for them but he pays a lot."

"Through a service?"

"No, I think he had a guy working corporate security or something. He took him on private and that guy built his team."

"Do you know his name?"

"Finnerich. Max Finnerich."

There's an image on the rim of my mind, fingernails inside a coffin. Buried alive, oxygen running out, no hope, no help, but an innate will to live. The body takes over when the mind shuts down. Out of options, cornered, left for dead, instincts take over. There is a bird, the godwit, that will fly from Alaska to New Zealand to nest, 7,000 miles, never having done it before.

Archie snaps me back to the moment. "Whatchoo thinking, Copeland? You want this Finnerich's number so you can arrange things?"

"No. Don't call him. Don't tell him I'm coming. Just give me an address."

Curtis looks between Archie and me. "That's it then?"

Archie shrugs. "The man says give him an address, you give him an address. You and me'll work out the business side of it later."

Curtis stands and Archie stands and I think about fingernails and instincts.

I've been in Portland before, a long time ago when I was first telling you my story and I was following a presidential candidate. I traveled south from Seattle, after meeting with my old fence at Sea-Tac Airport, because players in this game like to meet in airport terminals, on the other side of security monitors. No guns, no knives, everyone in the airport holding the same cards as everyone else. That was the last meeting I had with Vespucci before I killed his top hit man, Hap Blowenfeld, the assassin who brought me into the game. Nearly a decade has passed since I traveled the Pacific Northwest, since I helped my father end his campaign.

It is cold in Portland, but there's no snow on the ground, not like Mackinac. The sky is gray, the color of grave markers on a forgotten hill. Rain threatens, imminent, but is held back by the clouds, handcuffed, restrained.

I rent a gray sedan to match the sky, the buildings, the streets, so that it is as unnoticeable as a dry breeze. I park at a car wash on Southeast 82nd Avenue, hand my keys to the owner of the place, then grab coffee out of a metal dispenser inside a drab waiting area. The drink is surprisingly good, this car wash coffee. I wonder where he buys it, but then I remember I'm in Portland, and the coffee is superior here no matter where you get it. The owner stands at the glass, his back to me, watching my car roll through the auto-wash, and when it's finished traveling from one end to the other, he turns without a word and hands the keys back to me. In return, I hand him a thousand dollars in cash.

Once out of the lot, I pull to a side street and check the trunk. There's a blue duffel stuffed with weapons and ammunition, services arranged by Archie and provided by Suds Autowash, where rental cars are cleaned and traveling assassins can resupply without attracting the watchful eyes of law enforcement. I transfer the duffel from the trunk to the back seat and head out onto Interstate 5.

It's one in the afternoon.

I might as well get a jump on things and check out Matthew Boone's security detail. Archie offered to make a file for me, just like he would if Boone were my mark, but I declined. I want to observe his protection force in its natural habitat.

Boone's company is located downtown, next to the river. It takes up the top seven floors of a thirty-story building, with Boone's personal office on the twenty-ninth floor. The thirtieth, above it, is reserved for tech and infrastructure and servers and wires and systems and all the things we no longer think about when we turn on our computers. It serves the offices below.

I enter the lobby and walk over to a small security desk, manned by a bright-eyed, attractive, Irish woman—PEYTON, on her name tag. Late twenties, I'm guessing. Photos are taped to the inside of her counter, easy to spot from where I stand, fired employees who should not be allowed on to the elevator, I presume.

"Hello," I say with a bored but chipper aspect.

"Yes?" she answers.

"I have a meeting with . . ." then I allow a blank look on my face, "hold on, hold on," and I pull out my phone and start to swipe through a calendar. "The temp agency told me to remember specifically who I was subbing for and I *knew* I'd forget. I have it in an email. Hold on."

"What company?"

"Pop something?"

"Popinjay?"

"That's it."

She moves around her desk and over to a bank of elevators as she tugs on a key card attached to a chain around her neck. She presses the up arrow, and when the car doors open, she moves inside and waves the key card in front of a reader. Then she taps the button for the twenty-third floor. It lights up obediently. "Twenty-three," Peyton says with a smile. "That's reception."

Whatever illusion Boone holds that he's protected by putting his offices in a secure building with a secure elevator is about to shatter.

I step out behind Peyton as she returns to her desk. If I wanted to pop her, take her key card, and waltz to the twenty-ninth floor, I could. If this had been a real hit, maybe I would. Lucky Peyton.

She senses movement behind her and turns, puzzled. "Something wrong?"

"Are there stairs I can take? I have a bit of claustrophobia and honestly . . ." I pat my stomach, "I need the exercise."

"Twenty-three floors?"

"I don't mind." I show her all my teeth, and she returns a smile.

"Follow me."

I do, and she leads me to an unmarked door, swipes her key card again, pulls the handle, and holds the door for me.

"Good luck," she offers as I step inside.

The stairwell is a seldom-used, undecorated, utilitarian structure with metallic steps that switchback each half floor.

I pass the twenty-third floor in less than ten minutes and keep moving vertically. There are black credit-card-size swipe pads on each floor from twenty-four to twenty-nine, but as I hoped, the thirtieth floor has no such security.

I open the door and step out into an industrial maze of hot machines, tubes, wires, blinking lights, and data ports that only mean something to the manufacturer or repair technicians. The floor is finished, which is disappointing. I was hoping for the walking surface to be broken in places. I move among the machines, then kneel down and feel the tile with my fingers.

If this were a real hit, if I were here to kill Boone, I would know the layout of this floor, the precise square inch directly above his desk. I would work on the floor tile at night, unhindered, open a small hole above his chair, and—

The stairwell door clicks open behind me, and I feel the old blood thicken in my veins. I've only been here five minutes. Boone's security might not be so bad after all. I crane my neck, slowly, slowly, but can't spot any movement except the top of the door closing on its hydraulic hinge.

I shuffle two feet to my left to get a better view of who arrived on the floor behind me, and I'm surprised to see Peyton. She's not sweating, which means she's either in great shape or she took the elevator to the twenty-ninth floor and then ascended the stairs. Either way, she had eyes on me the whole time. She suspected me from the moment I stepped off the elevator. And if that's true, then—

The blow comes from my right, a devastating left hook delivered by a fist the size of a croquet mallet. My senses aren't as alert as they should be, so I catch the motion only a split-second before I see the constellation map explode behind my eyes. It is a good, clean hit, precise, aimed at my right temple, and it buckles my knees. I haven't been in a fight in a few years, and I'm out of practice. I'm not even trying to win. My battle is with consciousness.

My attacker follows with a kick to my ribs delivered by heavy boots, and when I crumple to my side to protect myself from the next blow, he uses my movement to flip me the rest of the way so I end up face down with his thick knee in the middle of my back. He must weigh 220, 230 lbs. The next thing he will do is try to get my hands behind my back so he can zip-tie them, which tells me he's law enforcement, a former cop, now working privately for Matthew Boone.

I'm guessing Max Finnerich, but how the hell should I know? If I'm going to do anything to flip this fight, I need to do it now.

I make my body limp, free of resistance.

With his knee for leverage, he uses both hands to secure my left wrist and pulls it back. I assume he's neutralized a lot of men this way over the years, though he's never neutralized someone like me.

The biggest advantage you can have in a fight is if your adversary thinks it is over. As his hands pull on my wrist, his weight shifts so he can rotate my arm, and that subtle shift in leverage is all I need. I throw my hips in the direction he is leaning and Newton's law kicks in and he can't stop his weight from pitching forward. With him off balance, I pivot my hips, and he has to let go to break his fall. I know this is coming, so I swipe his wrist before he can plant it and his face collides with the floor, his teeth rattle, and I drive a fist into his side for good measure, sapping his energy as I punch his lungs and cut off his oxygen. I didn't have to do the last part, but he kicked me.

Peyton, who has been watching from a few feet away, reaches for a taser attached to her hip, but my car wash Glock is out and up and pointed at her forehead. She freezes, her breath catching as she sucks in a lungful of air and is too frightened to let it back out.

Finnerich groans on the ground, disoriented, blood dripping from a busted nose. I catch movement over Peyton's shoulder, also on both sides of me, men attempting a flanking position, reinforcements joining the fray, using the cover of construction scaffolding to shield their attack.

I could kill every man and woman in this room. Peyton first with a head shot, Finnerich before he can clear the pinprick lights from his vision, then the two men hiding on my right, and finally, the man on my left as he panics and breaks for the stairwell door. I have no qualms about that much killing. I've done it before, more times than I can count, and I feel nothing for these men and this woman who hold deadly weapons but forget they've chosen a deadly profession.

But that's not my assignment. Not this time. Wives will get kissed, children held, and these bodyguards will live simply because I was hired to protect instead of to destroy.

In lieu of toppling all these dominoes, I lower my gun, put on an affected cocky grin like an actor playing to the dollar seats, and say, "Put your hands straight out in front of you." I advance a few steps toward Peyton, and the two men to my right signal the one on my left with all the subtlety of circus clowns. These guys. I should kill a couple just so the others can learn a terrible lesson.

I suppress that notion. *Let 'em come, let 'em come, let's get this over with.* A couple more steps and Peyton understands what the other men are doing and tries to maintain eye contact with me, and these amateurs are this close to offending me so completely that whatever happens, happens, and I can't be blamed. I mean, they're like elephants stomping around a windowless room. But what was I expecting?

Finnerich climbs to his hands and knees and screams a battle cry from his bloody mouth, and that's the signal his men have been waiting for. They fly from behind the scaffolding, tackle me, three on one, and I put up just enough of a fight to sell it, and then Finnerich looms over me while his three mutts pin my arms behind my back.

He spits blood on the floor in a sticky red wad, wipes his mouth with the back of his hand, makes sure to lock eyes with me, then raises his boot and kicks me in the head until my world goes dark.

—⚬—

They're holding me in a makeshift cell, presumably someone's office based on the cluttered desk and credenza. The blinds are drawn. I'm bound with plastic zip ties. Peyton plus the two men who tackled me stand guard. No sign of Finnerich, which is good. My guess is he's out explaining in person or over the phone to his boss what happened today. Another guess is his nose is pointing in a direction it wasn't pointed in this morning.

I make a show of regaining consciousness and test my restraints. Peyton watches warily, like a fisherman with an eye on the dark clouds bunching on the horizon.

"Can I get some water?" I ask.

The side of my head where Finnerich laid his boot is sore and swollen, and my lower lip is cracked, though the bleeding has stopped.

Peyton shakes her head.

I turn my eyes to Tweedledee, who has a red beard, and Tweedledum, who has narrow eyes. "Water?"

Peyton speaks up before they can answer. "Don't talk to him."

"Come on," I say, and look back at her. "I could've shot you in the face but I didn't. The least you can do is spare me some water."

Her eyes harden and her lips stretch tight. "If it were up to me, you'd be dead right now," she says flatly.

"Who would do it? You?"

"Maybe."

I laugh and it cuts through the room like a gust of northern wind. "With what? Your taser? They didn't even give you a gun."

"I'd have managed."

"Maybe you would have."

I study her now, squinting. I'm starting to like Peyton. She looks to be the most competent of the bunch. She's got some training . . . maybe military, maybe police.

"She your boss?" I say to the other two. The red-bearded one scoffs and says, "No."

"You sure about that?"

"I'm sure you should shut your fucking mouth until Mr. Finnerich gets back."

Peyton snaps at him, "Hey, moron. Did I just tell you not to talk to him?"

Red Beard frowns, sulky.

I laugh again and get the reaction I'm hoping for.

"Oh, is that funny?" Red Beard says, anger coming off him in waves.

I nod vigorously. "It is. Pretty much. Yeah."

Red Beard pulls out a Beretta from a shoulder holster and cocks it, crosses the ten feet that separate my head from his gun. Peyton jumps from her spot to get between us. "No, Carmichael. No."

He brandishes his weapon like he's going to use it as a sap, but Peyton stays in the way as the third dope keeps his spot holding up the wall.

"Get out of my way, Peyton," Red Beard, or I guess Carmichael, roars, but Peyton has both hands on his chest, like she's trying to hold a bullpen gate closed as Finnerich steps into the room.

"What is this?" he blasts from the doorway.

Carmichael stands upright and mutters, "Nothing," his face now a brighter shade than his whiskers.

Peyton lowers her eyes and adds, "Yeah, nothing."

I keep the smile on my face and train it on Finnerich, who has a butterfly bandage over the bridge of his nose and purple dashes under his eyes. Next to him stands a different man, one I haven't met yet. He's handsome, better dressed than anyone else, wearing tailored pants and an oxford shirt rolled up to the elbows. He's a few years older than I am, I guess, and his emotions are right on the surface: concern, fear, sure, but also a sense of relief. This is Matthew Boone, and he thinks the threat hanging over him was neutralized by his crackerjack team.

"Is this him?" he asks. "Is this the guy?" His voice can't mask his worry.

Finnerich holds up a protective hand, as though to say "I got this. Leave it to me."

He snaps his fingers at Carmichael and the wall-holder-upper as though they're trained German shepherds, and they step back to give him room.

"So," Finnerich says, and slides a chair over so the legs scrape the floor. "We're going to find a few things out about you, mister."

I assume he thinks this way of speaking, of holding his eyes, is frightening and cold. I wonder if he practices in front of a mirror.

He turns to Matthew Boone to dramatize his point and adds, "If anyone gets easily squeamish and doesn't want to look at what I'm about to do, then you should leave the room now."

No one moves.

Finnerich tosses a look my way to see if his threat made an impression, but I return half-mast eyelids to provoke him.

He swallows. This is getting fun.

He stands up and makes a show of taking off his shirt, flexing his muscles. He rolls his neck and ripples his biceps, his forearms.

All I can look at is his kneaded-dough nose, the damage irreparable. The thought of it keeps the smile on my face. Maybe I'll get another chance at it.

He threatens me again, something about what little is gonna be left of my face when he gets through with it, something about every bone in my body, and I really can't listen to any more of his blather, so I turn to the man in the doorway and say, "I take it you're Matthew Boone?"

"Don't answer that," Finnerich blurts, but apparently Boone isn't the kind of man who likes orders barked at him from his hired help, so he answers, "Yes. That's right."

"Okay, that's enough." Finnerich holds up a hand, reasserting himself.

I ignore the bodyguard, continue speaking directly to the boss: "Let me tell you all the ways your men fucked up today. One, I was allowed in the stairwell when I clearly had no reason to be in the building. Two, I was allowed access to the thirtieth floor, the one above your office. I could've easily gained entry to your ceiling from there. Three, your guards came at me with weapons but were not prepared to kill me or anyone else."

Finnerich wheezes as though I slapped him in the face. "Four, they all gave me their names . . . she is Peyton, he's Carmichael, he's Finnerich." I gesture at the narrow-eyed wall-holder-upper. "He's not important. Five, they told me you were coming. Matthew Boone. The big boss."

Boone steps toward me like he's navigating a museum crowd in front of a fine painting, trying to get a better look at me. He speaks, and his voice sounds more confident, like we're two friends trying to solve a math problem and he needs to correct my equation. "Okay, but here's where you're wrong—"

"Mr. Boone, don't—"

Boone holds up a hand to Finnerich, but talks to me. "Here's where you're wrong, friend. I wasn't in the building. I wasn't in my office. Even though you gained access to the thirtieth floor, even though you could've cut a hole in my ceiling, the problem for you is *I wasn't there*. You couldn't have reached me. I was at *home*. So maybe . . . just maybe these guys did exactly what—"

"You're here now."

He stops, confused.

Everyone's eyes circle at the same time.

With a speed no one in this room has ever witnessed, I shoot to my feet because they've zip-tied my wrists to the armrests but not my ankles to the legs, and this chair has a shallow seat with crossed legs for stability, which is fine when you're sitting but not so stable when someone is breaking it, and I whip around with my hips, plowing the leg tips into Finnerich's waist before he can mount a defense.

The legs snap and Finnerich reels and the plastic ties give or the armrests pop free or both, because all I have left dangling from my wrists are a couple of new plastic bracelets and my Glock is in my hand and pushed up against Matthew Boone's nose.

"You're here now," I repeat. And then I add, "*Ka-pow*," to bring it home.

3

I ride in the passenger seat of an Audi A8, the kind of car that usually has a professional driver in a blue sports coat behind the wheel, but Boone drives himself. He's relaxed since I told him I'm not the one sent to kill him but the one his friend Curtis sent to keep him safe. The fear that marked his face since he stepped into the office retreats. His hands are steady on the wheel. He doesn't wear a wedding band, I notice.

"You think I should fire everyone?" he asks casually.

"All I had on you was an address for your business and your home and a minimal description of your security detail. It took me less than an hour to have you up close and point blank at the end of my gun. I could have made the kill and gotten away with it. If this had been my assignment, if the name Matthew Boone had been at the top of my page, you would be dead right now. And here's the thing . . . if this had been real, I would've had a file on you listing the *best* places, the *best* times to find you the *most* vulnerable with the *least* amount of resistance. In other words, it would've been easier. Five minutes instead of an hour. The men you had protecting you couldn't do it even when I came at them directly. So, yeah, Max Finnerich isn't doing you any favors."

"Done," he says immediately. "I never really liked the guy anyway. He always acted like he was the smart one in the room. That he knew secret *things*. But he's a fraud so . . . done."

"I assume he hired the rest of the men."

Boone nods.

"Okay, they all have to go. You can't have cross loyalties."

"I understand."

"Except the woman . . . Peyton. Peyton on her name tag. She might be worth a damn. I don't know yet."

"You want to keep her?"

"For now."

"Whatever you want. You're the boss. Just tell me what I have to do, and I'll do it. I know there's a price on my head, and I know . . ." His knuckles tighten on the steering wheel. "And I know I've been scared out of my gourd for the last week and a half, but I guess I'm supposed to act normally so my business will run normally? Still, I feel like a metal target on a shooting range. Just sitting out in the open and at any moment, *plink, plink, plink*, someone's gonna knock me over."

He pauses and loosens his fingers, flexes them to drive the circulation back into the digits. "Sorry. I . . . this has been hard."

I know what it's like to be hunted, so I could offer him some comfort, but I don't know if he deserves it. The killer in me is accustomed to hating the target, finding something evil in him so I can exploit that evil when the time comes to kill him. That way, I can separate myself from the kill. Old habits die hard, I guess, because I'm already looking for things to hate about Matthew Boone, merited or not. I hate this ostentatious car. I hate that he's rich and he speaks to his employees like he's a class above.

This isn't my job anymore, to hate the target. It's not going to help me keep this man alive if I despise him. So why am I looking for these faults when I should be doing the opposite, finding reasons to support him?

"Why don't you start from the beginning?"

"Oh. Yeah. Okay, yeah," he says, raising his eyebrows and letting them fall in waves. "My hometown is San Francisco. I was born into a family that . . ."

"I meant the beginning of someone wanting to kill you."

"Oh. Right. Sure. That makes . . . that makes sense. Do you want the short version or the long version?"

"I got all night," I say.

—⁂—

"I was a coder for Apple in the heyday of Steve Jobs and the black turtlenecks and the iPad and a new release every year and lines outside the Apple stores all over America. I was right out of college and had a head full of ideas and not enough sense and my parents were poor and my job was a good job. My team worked on digital photo-organizational software, an application that allowed the user to collect and arrange photos, except we didn't call them applications at the time. We called them widgets then, but that name didn't stick with Apple fans.

"My team grew, and I moved up from coding to management, but I still liked to get my fingers on a keyboard, get my hands dirty. Oh, I'm sorry. That didn't come out right. Anyway, I liked to work. I didn't see myself as management. I hated meetings and schedules and committees and sales figures and all the reasons I went to MIT and not Wharton.

"I remember it clearly, the day I quit. I was looking over the code of a young developer, I don't remember his name, and his work was sloppy, full of errors, and I yelled at him. I said, 'I'm supposed to present this in two days!' I remember that. 'In two days!' And this kid looks at me like *this*."

He makes a stern face, his eyebrows in a V.

"Like he's pissed. Like I'm the enemy. *You're one of them.* And I thought, *Nope, no way. I'm not* them. *I'm us. It's us versus them and I'm definitely on the us side.*

"But I could see in this young coder's eyes that was not true. So I put in my two weeks.

"Sorry, this was going to be the short version. Okay, yes. So I put in my two weeks and I took a freelance programming gig but I thought to myself, *If I am them, then I might as well be them for* me. Does that make sense? I might as well start my own business and own my own code. If you want to make money in Silicon Valley, and I'm not talking about a salary, I'm talking about a number with a lot of zeros on the end, then you have to own the intellectual property.

"I'd been staring at photographs the entire time I was at Apple, and one thing stood out to me about pictures more than anything else. People took lots of pictures of faces. It seems obvious, but it was like a revelation to me. Sure there were landscapes or pictures of food or pets or tourist attractions, but more than anything, there were faces, day in and day out. Clothes would change, hairstyles, makeup, age, sure, but what I noticed mostly was sameness. The distance between the eyes, the size of the lips, the broadness of the forehead, the shape of the chin.

"I started to think about a code that could take two pictures of ten people and tell you exactly who each one is. This is number one and this is number two and way over here is number three and so forth. And then I thought about it on a massive scale. What if you could match a face on video footage with a preestablished database, say, of mug shots? This is after Timothy McVeigh. I wasn't even thinking about Muslim terrorists or anything like that. I had just reached a beta version of the software when 9/11 happened.

"The military came a-calling. They tried to buy me out but I learned from Steve Jobs to hold firm. Before I knew it, I had contracts with every acronym in the government—CIA, FBI, DHS, NSA—and when they decide they want something, they don't negotiate, they just pay. That's how I got rich.

"Facebook then came along and tried to buy me out, but I didn't back down from the FBI, so I wasn't gonna back down from Mark Zuckerberg. Apple eventually licensed some of my code and tried to improve on it, but their iPhoto software still sucks if you ask me.

"Okay, I'm going to wrap this up. I built Popinjay to about 200 coders and fifty project managers and another hundred support staff, and I kept it private and I run the big-picture macrobusiness side of it, but what I still really love doing is coding. It's like puzzle pieces inside a puzzle inside a puzzle inside another puzzle and the key to all of it is in an undiscovered foreign language. Okay, okay. Yes. You get it. I love it.

"So I shut myself in my office for hours at a time and I work on new software, and I came up with code that can scan millions of faces and find two alike in a nanosecond, from any angle, from any media, including a large swath of the web. I mentioned it to a reporter from *Wired* and he tweeted about it, and the next day all the alphabets were back on my doorstep plus representatives from ninety foreign governments on five continents, including some very eager buyers in the Middle East and Eastern Europe. You see—no covert intelligence officer would be able to hide his identity. In a matter of seconds, you would know if he or she were photographed at Harvard in 2002, Germany in 2004, Saudi Arabia in 2015. Lies checked. Surgeries necessary.

"It's only in beta, I tell everyone. It's not finished. But they want it anyway. They try to hack into my servers, at the office, at home. If I won't sell it, they'll try to steal it. But even if they got their hands on it, it would be meaningless to them. I've used symmetric encryption with a key system . . . anyway, the code would be gibberish.

"So I shut down any kind of negotiations until I knew *what* I had. Someone did not take kindly to that, apparently, because the FBI informed me that chatter indicates some foreign entity has ordered me killed. If they can't have it . . . they want no one to have it. And that's my story."

—⁂—

The boyish smile he keeps on his face as he tells it falls when he gets to the end of it, like a dog dropping its tail when he realizes his owner is calling for a bath rather than a walk. "Anyway, that's all I know. I have a friend who works in some dark places, Curtis, you know, and so I asked his advice and he made contact with you."

"What was the FBI's advice?"

"Witness protection."

"Why didn't you take it?"

"I don't trust them." He gives me a sideways look. "They want the software, too. I've seen the way they behave and I don't like it."

I nod. So have I but I don't need to tell him that. We're heading away from the city toward the suburbs and everything is green with houses set back from the roads. You only catch glimpses of wood and brick between the red alders, maples, and pines.

We turn onto a driveway and he punches a simple code into a keypad. An iron gate that looks like it wouldn't be much barrier to an SUV or light truck swings open. A dirt path disappears into a wooded rise, and we snake forward over it.

"Also," he says as he turns up a smooth drive, "I can't make them move."

The car twists around a cluster of firs and I see two boys tossing a football in lazy arcs. Their faces light up when they see the car and a cold hand grabs my stomach and twists it into a knot.

—⁓—

I sit in an armchair in the foyer, seething.

Boone is upstairs, talking on his phone in hushed tones, so I hear a low hum but can't make out the words. The intermittent sounds of laughter, squeals, thumps, and whistles reach me through a window as the boys, ignorant of danger, play toss in the yard.

The dirty bastard.

The dirty, foul-playing, son-of-a-bitch bastard.

I'm going to snap Archie's neck like a twig next time I see him.

He *knew.* He knew this idiot had a death threat on him and two boys at home that he hasn't even bothered to protect. He told me nothing about the boys. Nothing.

I stand as Matthew Boone returns from upstairs. "Sorry. Trying to steer a ship by remote is not what—"

I cut him off. "I can't help you."

"I'm sorry?"

"I can't take the job."

"Oh. I thought we were—"

"I suggest you upgrade your security and you take up the FBI's offer to relocate you and the boys until this blows over."

I stick out my hand and he shakes it, though he's still confused. "Okay, well, it was . . . good meeting you I guess. Can I drive you somewhere or call you an Uber?"

I shake my head. "I'll walk."

I head out without looking at the boys. I can feel their eyes on me as I step down the path. A hundred yards and I'm through the gate.

Two miles away, I find a gas station, buy a drop phone, and call Archie.

—⊶—

I pace.

Archie sits in a motel chair, his feet up on the small desk, a frustrating half grin on his face.

"You knew, you manipulative lying bastard. You knew this asshole had kids. Boys! You knew and you came to where I had a perfectly fine life and you ripped me out of there and you fed me this bullshit about two birds and the whole time you knew I'd walk into a house with three beds."

Archie flashes his broad smile and lights a Camel. "Perfectly fine? You practically tossed a noose over a ceiling beam."

"It was my *choice*!"

"To deal with your grief?"

"You're goddamn right."

"Well, you're dealing with it now."

"Don't. Don't you say her name, Archie, or I promise you you're not gonna like what happens next."

I'm so hot, I can't see straight. The room in front of me, the desk, Archie, they all swirl and swim like washing machine soap. There's a red edge to everything, like someone painted an angry border around my vision.

Archie sticks his cigarette in his mouth and holds up his hands, placating. "Fine. I won't say her name, but you gonna deal with this one way or another, because what you was doing wasn't dealing with it. It was the opposite of dealing with it."

"That's not for you to decide."

"Well someone needs to do it! You think I didn't want to burn down the world, myself in it, when Ruby died? You think I didn't go home and break every mirror in the joint so I wouldn't have to look at my reflection? Check and check. But I got up and I got back in it because *this* is the world we chose and we don't get to complain when it bites us."

I look down at my feet. My eyelids feel unnaturally heavy all of a sudden. My knees, my shoulders, my chest feel like gravity is pulling them through the floor. I fall into a chair. My fingers knead my forehead though they feel detached, like I'm watching someone who looks like me through the wrong end of a telescope.

"He's got boys, Archie," I plead.

"Yeah, he does. And they're gonna be on their own or dead if you don't help this man."

"I'm not a bodyguard, Archie. I'm a killer. I've been a killer since I was eighteen years old. You know that."

"That's true and it's not true. I know what lengths you've gone to protect someone."

My eyes flash at him and he looks away, like he's been scented by a dangerous creature and doesn't want to provoke it further.

"All I'm saying is you gotta work or you gotta go ahead and pitch yourself in the ocean, because what you've been doing these last two years? It ain't living. It ain't anything. My mom used to call it shuffling. It's *shuffling*. And it ain't worthy of you, Copeland."

I chew the inside of my lip and feel a twitch tug the corner of my left eye. Archie falls silent, fills an ashtray with butt after butt, and we sit that way a long time.

"He learns there's a price tag on his head and he doesn't isolate his boys?"

"He doesn't know better. You saw who he had helping him. They're all amateurs."

"Come on."

"I've seen plenty of people brilliant about some things and stupid as hell 'bout others. He knew the threat was enough to reach out to Curtis, but some part of his brain closed off the danger."

"How bad is it? Who is coming for him?"

"I'm working on that. In the meantime, he needs someone looking out for him and those boys. Keep everyone alive until I backchannel this shit, Copeland. That's what he needs. It's what you need, too."

I don't know how long he lets me shake my head, but eventually it melts into a nod.

Archie is the original smart bomb. I know he's manipulating me but he's impossible to resist.

"What do I do now?" I ask.

He stares at me with his head back, looking out over the tip of his nose, lining me up like crosshairs on a scope. "I'll take care of it," he says.

"I left without an explanation."

"I'll take care of it," he repeats.

—m—

I stand in the kitchen of Boone's suburban house, facing bay windows that gaze out over a small clearing in front of a line of trees.

Windows in homes are luxuries, installed for people without enemies. There's too much cover in the forest, too much darkness, too many shadows. I move away from the view without thinking about it. My feet work on their own, like neck hairs that stand on edge when the brain senses danger.

Boone enters and stutter-steps when he sees me.

"Guess I thought you left again," he says, then shakes his head. "Sorry about that. Your reservations were explained to me and I'm grateful you're back."

I nod, but that's all I can give him for now.

"Anyway," he continues, "I want you to meet Liam and Josh. Boys! Get in here."

The boys I saw tossing the football line up in front of me with somber, curious faces, like visitors at an open-casket funeral. They cluster under their dad's arms, tucking into either side of him. "This is Mr. Copeland. He's my new head of security."

"Boys," I say, because I can't think of anything else.

The younger one asks, "What happened to Mr. Finnerich?"

Boone stammers an answer so I help him out with, "Mr. Finnerich is out. He wasn't good enough to be the head of getting your dad's lunch order, much less head of security."

This gets a laugh from the smaller one, Josh. Liam continues to eye me cautiously.

"I liked him," he whispers.

"He wasn't your friend," I say. "And neither am I. I'm here to keep you and your dad safe, and that sort of requires me to be an asshole."

The boys flinch at the word and Boone works his jaw side to side as his cheeks flush.

Before he can say anything I beat him to the punch. "Anyway, now that we've met, good, do whatever I say when I say it and we'll get along like gravy on mashed potatoes. Otherwise, stay out of my way. I gotta talk to your dad now so you guys go upstairs and entertain yourselves."

The boys look up at their father for his blessing, confused. He taps them both on the shoulders and they rush away, grateful.

He steps toward me, anger rising. "Okay, you walked away once. Maybe you should again."

I return his stare, flat eyes, flat expression.

"They're just boys. You may not know how to talk to boys but let me tell you, it's not like *that*. Barking at them like some kind of rottweiler."

"Let me guess . . . Finnerich was their buddy? Used to swing them up on his shoulders? Piggybacks and cops and robbers and tag in the backyard? A real friend to them, huh? Well, that's how you end up standing over two gravestones, Mr. Boone. I get close, I get compromised, and people die. If I put eyes on them, I take my eyes off everything else. *Everything*." The edge in my voice is pointed, precise. I want him to hear me. I want him to flinch. "So I'm going to keep talking to them any goddamn way I feel like as long as I'm assigned to keep you alive."

Boone radiates heat, inflamed. I keep coming at him like a prizefighter scoring with my right, hooking him with my left. "First thing we're doing is moving you, all of you, to a secure location. Not your goddamn residence. Somewhere with zero connection to your personal life or your business. Once that's squared, we'll discuss how to take you off the grid completely."

"Lovely," he sneers. "And how am I supposed to run my company?"

"You won't. Not until this is over."

"And my children, Liam and Josh. They're not supposed to go to school?"

"That's right."

Boone snorts as if words aren't enough to convey his disapproval and so he'll speak in grunts.

There's a knock on the door and he jumps like someone poked his side with a thumbtack. Okay, that's good . . . maybe I've reached a part of his brain that understands the seriousness of the situation. I don't react. When someone comes for Boone, it won't be announced with a knock on the front door.

Before I get to the next room, the boys are already opening the door without so much as peeping through a window to see who is on the porch. Did Boone not tell them *anything*? He catches my look, reads my thoughts, and ducks toward the front door, but a woman is already entering the hallway.

"Peyton!" the younger boy laughs, excited, and she bends to allow him a hug. Stooped, she catches sight of me and her smile fades. She turns her eyes to Boone.

"You wanted to see me?" she asks him, straightening.

"I do," I answer for him.

—⁓—

We sit in a small office off the dining room, and though it has a window, we tuck in by a fireplace with no line of sight from the outside. She's trying to defeat her nerves by holding one hand in the other. Her eyes are bright, though, and she keeps them on me.

"You heard about Finnerich?"

"Yes, sir."

"What's your loyalty to him?"

"He brought me on three months ago and I'm grateful for that, but I don't owe him anything."

"You want to keep your job and protect Mr. Boone?"

"If you'll have me."

"How'd you get the job?"

"I was law enforcement for four years, down in Los Angeles, two years in the sheriff's department, which was truly awful, then two years foot patrol in mid-Wilshire, which was always an adventure. I dug it. Pay was good but I was always up against it. I got a brother with some health problems so I helped out there. I met Finnerich during a firearms class he was teaching to the LAPD with Carmichael. They'd bring in tac guys from other police departments around the country to do specialty training seminars, I'm not sure why. Carmichael, he was the one with the red beard. He put the moves on me after class. I think Finnerich liked the way I said 'no.'

"Months later, when he'd gone private and Boone hired him to put a team together, he remembered me. Offered this job at forty an hour plus room and board, month to month with a two-month buyout when the job ended. I figured, *Why not*? I could use the money and if it worked out, it worked out. It seemed like something different. I'd never been up here before."

She stops and tries to read my thoughts.

"You're not married?" I ask.

"No, sir."

"Children?"

"No, sir."

"Dating? Love life? Sleeping with anyone?"

She doesn't blush. "No, sir."

"You ever fire your weapon on patrol?"

"Yes, sir."

"When?"

"A year ago. Two men were caught with fifty keys of heroin in a trap in the back of an old Cadillac. They fled and I pursued. The big one tried to ambush me in an alley. I opened up on him, caught him in the chest, and he went down. The other got away."

"You kill him?"

"No, he recovered. Long enough to stand trial, at least. Got convicted. After that, I don't know."

"How'd you tell him 'no'?"

"I'm sorry?"

"You said Finnerich hired you because he liked the way you told Carmichael 'no.' How'd you tell him 'no'?"

She leans back, and for the first time, she smiles.

She opens her mouth to answer, and I lean forward to hear it, but before she can tell me the story, one of the kids screams from somewhere above us.

4

Time is the world's greatest con man, the devil to Faust, Loki the trickster, the cruel, clever beggar who shows you an apple but gives you poison. When you crave time, when you plead on your knees for it, when you'd trade everything you own for one single minute, it gives you the back of its hand.

When you wish time would pass quickly, when you need it to hurry, when you need it to have mercy on your suffering, it stretches and yawns, a cat in a sunbeam, lazy and indifferent.

And when you think you have a surplus of it, when you push it to the background and believe it's not a factor, there's no need to hurry, you find that time has other plans.

I am up and out of my seat like a sprinter out of the blocks and though I don't know the layout of the house, I race toward the sound of that scream, not a play scream, a terrified scream, find a staircase, and I'm up it two steps at a time, making too much noise but I'm not here to kill, I'm here to protect I have to keep reminding myself, and a lot of noise can be a deterrent, a tiger's growl, an elephant's trumpet.

I crash through a bedroom door and the older boy, Liam, holds his brother, who points out a window. "I saw two men with guns," he says as his father enters the room.

"What were they wearing?"

"Black pants, black jackets, black rifles, like machine guns."

I don't have to wonder how a ten-year-old can identify weapons. Kids these days scroll through detailed arsenals in their first-person-shooter video games. He could probably tell me what brand of rifle if I asked.

Instead, I address Matthew Boone. "All three of you in the closet, now. Push as far back as you can and cover yourselves with clothes. Anything you can find. Do not come out even when you think it's over. Do not come out for anything except my voice. I will come get you, and that's when you respond. Understand?"

Boone nods, his face ashen. He gathers his boys like a bulldozer scooping gravel, herds them into the closet, and shuts the door behind him. I hear rustling as they nest inside, followed by silence. Good. I know he'll listen in a crisis. I could stay in this room and hope to pick the riflemen off when they make their move, but this isn't the Alamo and I'm not defensive by nature. I'm the sword, not the armor.

Quickly, silently, I duck out of the room and check a window that aligns with the side of the house. The sun shines from the west so I'm sure the glare will give me a view without extending the two men the same courtesy. They chose dusk to make their assault, which speaks to how little they respect Boone's security. I hope the intelligence they gathered before this gig was only up to date to yesterday, when Boone employed a man named Finnerich to protect him. If so, they're going to have a rude awakening.

I hear glass tinkle in the back of the house and a door creaks open, somewhere off the kitchen, maybe the back hallway where the Boone boys toss their dirty shoes, snow boots, and raincoats. These men are confident if they don't mind being spotted by a boy out a bay window or announcing their entry with broken glass and a noisy door. They are either inexperienced or far too relaxed, but it's clear they are not ready for me.

I don't like the stairwell as an attack zone, far too many rails and a thick wooden banister that might provide cover, so I descend, feather-footed, and push back from the wall so I'll have a chance to pop out before they know what hit them.

Motion in my periphery and I turn to see Peyton peering back at me from her own ambush position on the other side of the sofa. I haven't forgotten about her, but I wasn't expecting her to engage. She nods at the left-most hallway and I'm glad she does. There are two ways to get to this staircase and I figured I had a fifty-fifty chance of choosing correctly, but would adjust if I rolled snake eyes. Peyton just slipped me loaded dice.

I nod back at her, grateful, and she raises two fingers for two intruders. I signal to her to get down but she shakes her head, so I give her a stern, *right fucking now*, all-business glare and this time she gets the message and lowers her head below the sofa.

Footfalls echo on the red oak floor of the left hallway, and I time it so that they'll be big targets and swing out with my Glock in firing position. They're walking side by side, which means this really is an amateur parade, and I can see in their eyes and by their rifle muzzles pointed at the floor that they are not prepared for armed response, much less one that doesn't call out "Wait!" or "Freeze!" or "Hold up!"

I blitz both of their faces, the first shot through the bridge of the intruder on the left's nose, so his head caves in on itself. My second shot catches his friend's eye, blows out the back of his head, and Jackson Pollocks the wall behind him. Two men enter, two men dead.

My adrenaline subsides but it was satisfying to feel it again. I calmly move to inspect the raiding party, though I don't need to kick their legs or poke their shoulders with the barrel of my gun. I know they're dead. That's what headshots do for you, take out the guesswork.

Something feels wrong. I've tussled with a wide range of body-guards and a handful of killers and these two fall on the wrong side of the bell curve for talent. They didn't split up, they barged in from the outside with all the nuance of a marching band, and they had their rifles pointed at the floor like they'd have all the time in the world to use them.

I feel Peyton approach behind me.

"Is it over?"

"For now." I rifle through their pockets.

"What're you doing?"

"I'd like to find out who they are, who they work for. Most hit men or hit crews wouldn't carry personal information on them but this isn't much of a crew so maybe we'll get lucky."

The first guy's pockets are empty. I hear scuffling upstairs and know the tension has gotten the better of Boone and he's stirring.

"Should I go tell them they're all clear?"

"No," I respond. "This is good training for them. Grab the quilts on the sofa, and let's cover these guys so the boys don't have to see them."

She looks at me funny and I already regret showing sympathy. But she hops to it before I change my mind.

In the second guy's pocket is a handwritten map of this house, arrows and squiggly lines to indicate entry points, stairwells, bathrooms, bedrooms, closets. It's fairly well-detailed, if useless. A few places have words printed on them in blocky masculine letters: master bedroom, boy's room, boy's room, that type of thing.

Another thump upstairs and I look up the stairwell. I make a mental note to talk to Boone about all the noise he's making. He may as well have a field radio and call out his position.

Peyton returns with the quilts, and spots the drawing in my hands. "What's that?"

I show it to her.

"Someone drew these guys a map."

Her face snaps white, then red, as the blood leaves then flushes her cheeks, a tide of emotion. She looks at me and sucks in air, then says, "I recognize that handwriting."

—᭝—

Boone says so many thank yous I have to stop him before I lose all respect for him, what little there was to begin with. The kids look shell-shocked and though I don't need them seeing horrors that will keep them up at night the rest of their lives, I make sure we pass by the quilt-covered bodies on our way out of the house. The younger one, Josh, eyes the wall where gravity worked the blood into streaks.

I snap my fingers a few times so I gather all eyes to me.

"Peyton, you have a car big enough to fit all of us?"

Boone speaks up, trying to be helpful. "I have a Range Rover."

"Nothing tied to you."

"Ahh," he manages and lowers his head with one hand raised like he gets it and won't interrupt again.

Peyton speaks up. "I have an SUV. A Ford."

"Bring it around to the side of the house. There. Hop into the passenger side and keep the engine running."

She nods and is out the door, head on a swivel.

The boys' eyes are glazed, blocking out the world, one of the brain's many defense mechanisms. If you can't see it, you can't feel it. Except that's not true, not really. Another of time's tricks. Horrors you think are buried deep in the past pop out of the darkness, fresh and dusted off, like only seconds have passed. The boys will come to grips with that truth soon enough. I'm not here to comfort them, although their father looks too rocked to provide much succor. I'm not paid to comfort. That's his job.

I level my eyes at him. He's scared, and that's better for me. "Keep doing what I say and we'll come out of this on the other side."

"Yes. I will. Thank you."

"You carrying a phone?"

He nods and hands it to me.

"What about the boys?"

The older one, Liam, nods, forks it over.

"You?"

Josh shakes his head. "Next birthday."

I move to the fireplace and toss their phones into the flames. No one protests. They're in new territory, and their survival instincts engage.

I drive toward Portland while I connect with Archie on my phone. We've always had a shorthand, and a few sentences inform him there's already a body count, and I have Matthew Boone and the children with me, looking for a safe house. Archie agrees to call me back and in less than ten minutes he does, with directions northeast to Cedar Creek Road.

We follow them until we arrive at a furnished farmhouse with a key under a brick on the porch. What arrangements he made and how fast he made them astounds me. I'm sure he was looking for real estate as soon as he set this job for us, but I am always surprised by how well he anticipates my needs. He really is the best fence in the business.

The farmhouse is nice, set back from the road and positioned on top of a grassy knoll with views from a wraparound porch that might as well be from turret towers. The furniture is rustic, a lot of leather and animal horns, and there are a half dozen bedrooms and bathrooms. I'm sure it's a rental, and that Archie paid a lot of cash to get the key with no questions. No one knows we're here, and Archie will have used enough middlemen to keep it that way. The refrigerator is stocked, there's firewood cut and stacked in a log rack, and there are plenty of warm blankets and quilts.

Boone disappears with Josh and Liam upstairs, presumably to choose beds, but he doesn't return and I hear muffled conversation drifting from above. Whether he's selling them lies or telling them the truth, I don't know.

Peyton looks at me, hands on her hips. "I saw a coffeemaker if you want to split a pot."

"Sounds good."

She goes to work. After a moment, she calls out, "We never got around to it, but I want to say I'm very interested in the job if you still want me."

I can't help but smile. "I figured you'd hightail it out of here now that you've seen how it works."

"You'd let me?"

"I wouldn't stop you."

"But I know where this house is."

"I trust you," I say, and I mean it. Trust for me has always been instrumental in the way I conduct my business, and Peyton's behavior

59

during the siege says more than anything she could say with her mouth.

"Well, I want the job and I'm gonna reward that trust."

"I bet you will."

I tell her Archie will work out the compensation details, assure her she'll be taken care of, and she takes the information unconcerned. Money has never been important to me either. I got into this because I am good at it, and the part I only admit to myself when the lights are low is I like the power of killing. I've been doing it since I was very young, professionally since I was nineteen, and all it cost me was everyone I ever loved.

Peyton asks me something but I miss it because the past is threatening to overwhelm me again and although I know how to arm myself against it, I find I'm inured to its call. I bathe in it now. I swim in it. I drown in it.

The way I die is strangulation, choking on memories.

"I'm sorry, what?"

"Are we in this alone?"

I nod. "You, me, and Archie."

"What do I call you?"

"Copeland."

"Is that a first name or a last name?"

"Take your pick."

"Okay, Mr. Copeland. Do you mind telling me what you want me to do?"

"I want you to stay here and put two bullets in anyone who walks through the door. If Mr. Boone asks to contact the outside world, you politely decline."

Boone speaks up from the stairwell. "I won't. Try to contact anyone, I mean." He steps into the room just as Peyton takes the pot off the burner. She nods at the coffee and he nods back, so she adds a third mug to the counter and pours us each a cup. I blow on mine, take a sip, and it's strong and delicious. I don't know if the owners left it or Archie stocked it, but tip of the cap to whoever did.

"The boys are asleep," Boone continues. "I think. I'm not sure actually. But I wanted to come down and thank you again and see what I can do to help. And to let you know . . . I'll do—and the boys will do—whatever you tell us."

"For now, you're doing it. Stay here, don't leave the property. Don't call anyone, don't email anyone. Keep Peyton with you."

"You're leaving?"

I nod and drain the last of my coffee.

"Where are you going?"

I set the cup down and it rattles until it's still.

"Better to read about it later," I say, and head out the door.

—⁂—

I find him a few blocks from the apartment he rents downtown. The sky is a quilt, dark and light patches sewn together randomly, no comfort in the chaos, no acknowledgement from the sun. Let it hide.

I'm in position to put eyes on the address Peyton gave me when I spot Max Finnerich at the window counter of a nearby sandwich shop, chewing on a Philly cheesesteak, anxiously checking his phone for messages, holding it to his ear to leave stern voice mails. His nose still has the twin butterfly bandages holding it together, boxer's dressings. I look across the street to where an ATM is affixed to a wall, and now I know why he's sitting here, in this window, at this counter. He wants a time and date stamp of where he was when the murder took place, and the ATM camera will provide it.

He looks worried, and he should be. His eyes drift outside to the street without seeing anything, his face as easy to read as a bargain bin thriller. He's trying to get an update from the two amateurs who were gonna take out Matthew Boone, and presumably, they've missed the report time. He didn't have a plan B, and his world is unraveling in front of him. He should've taken his severance and walked away, but I bruised his ego along with his nose in Matthew Boone's office, and he wants a do-over.

Finnerich looks at the phone's face again, desperate for news, but it tells him nothing to assuage his fears. He tosses half his sandwich into a nearby trashcan, absently puts on his jacket and folded watch cap, and heads out the door. I face the window of a clothing store and watch him in the reflection of the glass as he trudges up the street back toward his apartment, hands stuffed in pockets, cheeks red though not from the cold. He doesn't look in my direction.

I know where he's going so I don't have to risk alerting him to my position. After five minutes, I follow.

In the hallway outside his apartment door, I wait. There's only one other door on this floor, and if someone enters or exits it, I'll act like I'm delivering a package. I figure Finnerich is too jumpy to stay long anyway. In this job, you have to have patience. I could kick in his door, but I don't know what's on the other side, so I decide to—

The door opens and before Finnerich can register his surprise, I rear back and kick him in the chest, sending him pinwheeling back into his apartment, arms spinning like fan blades, until he falls on his back. The black duffel he was holding, presumably his go-bag, parachutes away from him and bounces across the floor. His bewilderment turns to comprehension quickly, his eyes widen, and he twists onto his stomach and elbow crawls toward the bag. I kick the door shut behind me then spring across the room, drop a knee into his back, and pinch my Glock to the back of his head. He freezes, three feet away from his duffel, and raises his hands so that only his chest, waist, knees, and toes touch the ground.

"Don't shoot, don't shoot!" he cries, his broken nose making it sound absurd. I get up, take a few steps back so I'm clear of lunging distance, and keep my gun aimed at his head.

"Roll over."

He does, eyes sweeping hysterically but finding no salvation within reach. The bandages on his nose have slipped off on one side so they're flapping like birds with busted wings. The wound I put there is open again.

"Please, I'm sorry. I messed up and I'm sorry," he blubbers.

"Who paid you?"

He looks genuinely confused. It gives me pause, so I try again. "Who were the guys at Boone's house?"

"Were?"

"The men who paid you for the map and address?"

"What?" Things clear for him. I can see understanding flood over him in a wave. "Wait. They didn't *pay* me. I sent them. I wanted to show Mr. Boone—I wanted to show him what a big mistake he made getting rid of me. You got in his ear and messed with his head and he made a mistake. So I sent Steve and Tony to, you know, bust you up, show him you were nothing. That *I* was his guy. Not you."

A new thought arrives. "Oh, God . . . what'd you do to them?"

"They're dead."

His face twists into anguish, suddenly and violently. He starts bawling, sobbing with enormous wretches, so incongruous with the tough-guy demeanor he affected when he thought he was going to give me a beat down in the Popinjay offices when he took his shirt off and preened like a gamecock.

"No. No. No no no no no no," he wails, and his broken nose drips and splashes onto the floor.

"Hey. Hey!" I snap with my free hand to try to bring him back.

"No," he blurts. "No! You did not kill them. You did *not*. They were just kids." He sounds like a child throwing a tantrum.

"Actually, they were adults with guns."

"They weren't going to hurt anyone. Just you. But they weren't going to—oh, God!" The last bit comes out in a spray of spittle.

There was a time in my life when I would've killed this guy for making the mistake he made, trying to play a game way out of his league. He was a security professional, where men hit punching bags and shoot paper targets and wear dark sunglasses and parade around in tight muscle shirts and think the girls at the bar will flip. He probably likes the way his broken nose looks in the mirror, what it is going to do for his exaggerated stories sucked up by the barflies at the Pig N' Whistle, especially when the fantasy was going to end with him winning back his job after scaring me away.

"They were just kids. They were my sister's kids." He looks pathetic and distraught and harmless and I believe him. I move to the kitchenette, grab a towel off the refrigerator handle and wet it in the sink, all while keeping one eye on Finnerich. He sits where I left him, blubbering like a two-year-old. I've seen men cry before, but never like this. I throw the towel at him so it hits him in the chest. He catches it in his lap, so I tell him to clean himself up. He holds the towel to his face and cries harder, body shuddering with each sob. I'm getting annoyed.

I loom over him, and when he lowers the towel, I crack him in the cheek with the flat of my hand. He yelps and then glares at me with unmasked hatred. At least he's stopped crying.

"Listen up and don't say a word because I'm gonna lay out for you your next few years." His breathing slows, and though his anguish hasn't subsided, he's paying attention. "First of all, the two bodies will be taken care of. If you go looking for them, you won't find any sign they existed. There won't be bodies in caskets at a funeral, there won't be homicide investigators, or bullets pulled out for forensics.

You think you know something about me? You wanna know more? Curiosity burning through you right now? I can tell you that you know less about me today than you did yesterday and you'll know less again in a week, and when my face comes back to you every now and then in the quiet moments of the future, and you try to push it away."

He continues to glare at me as the wheels in his thick skull try to keep pace with the conversation, but I'm not sure he can get there. Or maybe I just want to keep him dizzy, off-balance. It's an old habit I fall into whenever I deal with people who aren't as smart as they think they are.

"Now you're asking yourself, what do I do next? I have to tell my sister her sons are dead, right? I will leave that to your discretion, but this is where two paths diverge in the woods. There's one path where you cop to what you know and the questions grow exponentially difficult to answer. Your sister will ask how you know and you'll tell her because you sent them to rough me up and there will be no evidence, just two missing grown men and your sister with more questions than you'll ever be able to answer.

"Then there's another path for you. It'll be hard at first, but will grow easier in time. This path is where you play dumb, where you say you have no idea what your nephews were up to, where every response is denial, and you'll be the only one who ever knows the truth. On that path, there's hope for you. Hope that doesn't end with you dead or in jail.

"You can choose which path to take. It's irrelevant to me."

He wipes blood and snot off his face with the towel but hate still burns in his eyes.

"Okay, I see the third path you're thinking about, the one where you come after me, or Matthew Boone, or Boone's family, or any number of revenge fantasies that'll pop up from time to time in your head. Let me tell you what's at the end of that path. This."

I nod at the Glock in my hand. "If Matthew Boone or I ever see you again, I will kill you, your sister, your mother and father, and any other person you ever loved. Look at me. I've done it before and I'll do it again. I am not exaggerating. Your whole life, you've never met someone like me."

The light goes out in his eyes.

"I'm going to walk away from here and you won't ever see me again. I don't know if it's in a week, or a month, or two months, but I suggest you get out of Portland, just so we don't accidentally bump into each other."

I don't bother giving him another minute, turn, and walk out the door.

—⚊—

I used to hold no pity. I used to make people pay for their mistakes. So have I evolved or devolved?

I'm in unchartered territory here, and I have been since Risina died on a covered bridge in Massachusetts and Pooley left with Jake. Archie shined a light on it when he tracked me down for this job offer, when he asked me to protect instead of subtract, and if his plan is to get me back in the game any way he can so I'll kill for him again, I'm not sure he thought this through.

I call him and let him know I've taken care of Finnerich but not "taken care of him."

Archie answers with a "Hmm," but I let it go.

5

Peyton and I walk the perimeter of the farmhouse twice a day. I look forward to the ritual. Archie said he needed at least a week to get the information we need, so I settle in to play defense until the ball switches ends.

I'm not built this way, waiting for someone to come to me, but I'm adapting. Evolution or devolution?

"Why don't you talk to the kids?" Peyton asks.

"That's not my job."

"Okay, but they're lovely. The older one, Liam, he's scared but he doesn't want to show it. He's always got a smile on his face, always a 'How are you' or 'Thank you' or a 'That's so cool.' And the younger one, Josh, he's a lion. Just when you think—"

"Stop."

"I didn't mean to—"

"I don't want to hear about the kids. I don't want to hear about the dad or the kids or you."

"Well that's shitty."

I grimace, but she digs in.

"It is. You wanted the job. You had no problem waltzing in and taking it and now I've watched you, I helped you kill two men who meant to kill us, so we're bonded as far as I'm concerned. That's just how it is."

"Peyton," I say curtly.

She touches my arm, "You're going to tell me about you and I'm going to tell you about me and there's nothing to argue about because that's what we're doing."

I glare and so she continues before I can interrupt, "Or . . . or you don't have to talk about you, fine, whatever, but you're going to listen to my story."

"Fine."

"Fine?"

"I'm not gonna stop you from talking."

"That's right. You're not. You're not gonna stop me. Because I actually care about keeping this family safe, and since it's your job, too, I care about you. So listen to my story and maybe that will give you a reason to care about me."

I know that no matter what she says, she's not gonna get the response she craves, but it's not worth arguing anymore. If she wants to spill her guts and eat into our waiting time, I won't stand in her way.

THE WAY I DIE

I'm a sucker for a good story, you know that well if you've followed me this far, so maybe I'll get lucky and Peyton will tell a corker. If not, maybe time won't be the only thing I have to kill.

"Okay, let's hear it. For the love of God, anything to get you to stop talking about your feelings."

We continue our loop around the house.

Smoke puffs black from the chimney, so we know Boone and the kids are up and he's made a fire. I look over at Peyton to see if she's reacting to what I said or the way I said it, but no, she's deciding where to start.

—⁓—

My father was a drunk, but a happy drunk. A kind of jolly, fat Santa Claus who made every room happier when he was in it, even if his cheeks were a little red or his words a little slurry. He came from Kerry, Ireland. His dad was a soldier and expected my dad to follow in his footsteps, but my dad's footsteps crossed the Atlantic and then the United States all the way to Los Angeles and never took him back. He settled in Los Feliz and opened a candy store making buttermints or what we called soft candy, which is a lot like salt water taffy. I don't know, they're hard to describe.

I've never found any other sweets that tasted like my dad's and believe me, I've looked everywhere. So, he starts this candy store and for a while, it goes well. He meets my mom at a dance bar in Maravilla, and she's still got her figure at this point, the way she tells it, and he's in love with her before the jukebox switches from A-8 to B-9. She liked his mustache, and the sweet smell that seemed to come out of his pores, and the way he'd always have a light sprinkling of sugar on his cheeks. She had no money, and he was doing all right, and he was her ticket out of a too-crowded house. That old tune that's been played a thousand times.

Were they in love? My father was. That I know. But he also loved his liquor, and if he had to choose one over the other, I can't say I know which way that vote would go.

Did she love him? She told me she did. At least for a time. It's all mixed up with what happened later.

69

That's called foreshadowing, Mr. Copeland. You'll have to wait for it because I don't give it up all at once. Do I have you? I do. I can see it. I'll give it to you nice and slow so you're wanting more. Ha, I'm just messing with you. Don't give me that look. Fine, back to the sad tale of Mr. and Mrs. Paddy Martin. That's my last name by the way, Martin. Peyton Martin.

Four months after their wedding night, they had me, which tells you everything you need to know about that, and four years later, they had my little brother Bartley. Bart. I call him Bartley but he wants to go by Bart. Fine. Whatever. His name, his call, but he'll always be Bartley to me.

My dad wanted a big family, but Bartley must've wrecked things coming out of the womb because mom couldn't get pregnant after him. At least that's what she told him, but I have a distinct memory of getting in her purse once and finding this clamshell compact and surprise, surprise, there's candy inside and my mom catches me and swats the clamshell violently out of my hand and across the room and tells me she'll wear out my behind if I ever get in her purse again, so yeah. My dad wanted a big family and my mom had other ideas, so she was on the pill and telling him her doctor said she couldn't make any more babies. This crushed my old man but I was too little to understand it at the time.

He stopped hiding his drinking, brought bottles home after work, and drained them in front of the TV, watching soccer on Eurovision until he passed out. My mom is still young at this point. She's got two kids under ten and a husband who stops giving her whatever she thought she was promised when they said "I do." Mom starts staying out late, meals stop getting made, first dinners, then breakfast.

Dad's response is to stop drinking. I don't know if it was the wake-up call he needed, but he snapped out of it like the lights had come on in a dark theater. I didn't know it at the time, but he went to meetings, he went to church, he committed to it, all twelve steps, all of that. The way he tells it, mom gave him the ultimatum he needed. The only problem was this didn't play out the way my mom wanted.

She had just begun to see a life for herself that didn't involve a husband, much less kids who were growing like weeds, and she had the perfect excuse to escape as the heroine of her life story . . . a drunk husband who couldn't satisfy her.

For a month, things settled to normal. Still, she found excuses to go out to dinner, to drink with her girlfriends, to take weekend trips out of town. At eight years old, I only vaguely knew what was going on, and to be honest, I was just glad to have my dad back, smelling like candy instead of the bottle, his big mustache tickling the side of my neck when he hugged me.

He took over all the house duties, got us fed, got our teeth brushed, got us tucked in, told us bedtime stories, and then went down the hall to an empty bed.

You think you know where this story is going, but you don't. You want to know why I became a cop? You're about to find out. Bet you didn't see that one coming. I see that hint of a smile, Mr. Copeland. Okay, fine.

My mom didn't come home for a full week, and my dad snapped. He didn't go back to drinking, he didn't pick up a gun or anything, but he snapped, like the buttons holding his feelings together just popped all at once. He told me to watch my brother, he had to go out for a bit, he had to set something right, and I remember crying and telling him not to leave because I had a feeling something was going to go very wrong, but he was in a fog, and he just brushed away my arms like a cow's tail twitching at mosquitoes. When he closed the door behind him, I wailed, my brother wailed, we both wailed enough to wake the neighbors, but this was a building where no one stuck their necks out for anyone else.

After a while, my tears were all gone and Bartley was sleeping and I made myself a bowl of cereal and waited for the door to open again. I remember looking at that door, willing it to open and for my father to walk through with a couple of buttermints for Bartley and me, smiling, and smelling sweet.

The next one through the door, though, was an LAPD officer, a good-looking Hispanic man with shiny teeth and a dimple in his chin. He told me to gather up a night bag for my brother and me, his name was Miguel, he was a friend of my mother's, and he'd be helping us. He had a friendly smile and gentle eyes and it seemed inevitable that this was going to happen, that a policeman was going to enter our lives.

I asked what happened and he said our mother would explain to us but to please hurry. I remember the ride in the back of the police car, the twenty minutes that seemed to last forever, the mesh net built into the glass divider, the door handles that didn't work from inside. All the time, I looked at the back of this big, strong man's head, neck, and shoulders as he drove and he cracked jokes and asked us questions about ourselves and tried to make this horrible situation just a little less horrible.

We arrived at the police station and they shepherded us into a room down a hall that looked like someone's office but there wasn't anyone inside. A sergeant came by and gave us some sandwiches and sweatshirts to cover our pajamas and left. Miguel came too and made us feel better with a smile, but the whole time I was thinking that this was the end. I wasn't going to see my mom or dad again. I wondered how it worked. Would I go to an orphanage? Would Bartley and I get split up? I just didn't know how any of that worked, so I was terrified.

I asked Miguel what was happening and I think he was about to answer when my mother walked in with a huge bandage on her head and her blouse soaked with blood and she hugged Bartley and me fiercely and said everything was going to be okay and I remember crying and saying, "Where's Dad, where's Dad, where's Dad?" but she rocked me and said "Shhh, shhh, it's gonna be okay," and I could smell the blood on her blouse as she hugged me to her chest.

The trial was short.

My dad had attacked my mom with a knife from the candy shop, cut her deep in the head. Miguel, the police officer, had been nearby and heard her scream and pulled my dad off my mom before he could hack her again.

My dad did not take the stand. Miguel and my mother testified against him and he was sentenced to twenty years in prison. Miguel and my mother, the hero cop and the damsel in distress, fell in love, and as soon as the divorce was finalized, got married.

He treated Bartley and me as if we were his own children, and mom settled down again, happy for the first time in years.

My brother and I were raised under Miguel's roof and everything stabilized.

—⁂—

"So you were wrong," I say.

"How so?"

"You said I wasn't going to see where this story was going, but you telegraphed it a mile away. Your surrogate father cop raised you and you followed him into the police force when you came of age."

Peyton stops and frowns. "Did you hear me say, 'The End'?"

"I guess not."

"Did you hear me say they lived happily ever after?"

"No."

"What kind of storyteller would I be if this were it?"

"Not a very good one."

"Then will you shut up and give me some credit?"

I grin and raise my eyebrows. "My mistake. Continue, please."

"Are you going to interrupt me again?"

I assure her I'm not, so she continues.

Okay, so you thought I was gonna say we lived happily ever after, but I've found that doesn't happen in life. Life lulls you into thinking everything's gonna work out and when your defenses are down, when you're at your most vulnerable, that's when life hauls off and knocks you on your ass.

I had a hard time lining up the man who viciously attacked my mother with the man I remembered getting himself sober, cleaning up after us, changing Bartley's diapers, turning his life around. The man I knew who literally smelled like sugar day in and day out and had never lifted a hand to anyone just couldn't have done the things they said he did in the trial. Now I know that people get drunk and do stupid things, but I also learned about passing the smell test. Have you heard that one? It means if you think something smells funny, trust your nose.

I asked to visit my dad in prison a few times in the early years, but mom refused to take us to Corcoran, so I stopped asking. He sent me mail during that time, but my mom burned the letters. I didn't find that out until much later.

So I went on living and pretended to my mom and Miguel that I stopped thinking about my dad.

But I never stopped.

Every time I ate dessert, every time I smelled something sweet, I would feel his mustache tickling my neck.

Like life, I wanted to lull my mom into security, into a fog, let her think that I wasn't thinking about him, that I'd forgotten him, that I loved my new existence as she did and had no need to complicate it. I got my driver's license at seventeen and saw on the Internet it was 337 miles to Corcoran. I also discovered I had to be eighteen to see my father without a chaperone, so I had a year to plan how to make it happen.

I befriended a girl, Donna, who lived on the other side of town, a good girl who got straight As, the kind of girl your parents encourage you to befriend. I didn't go to parties, I didn't go to sporting events, I didn't date boys, I kept my grades up, I didn't do anything to get in trouble or betray Miguel and mom's trust. For all they knew, I was a model daughter.

About halfway through the school year, I started spending the night at Donna's house and I made sure to leave my phone on in case they were checking GPS to see if I was where I said I was. I know they looked at my texts too, so I kept everything clean and even dropped in a little disinformation—my mom is *so* kind, Miguel is a *great* dad, that kind of thing. And the lulling worked. Bartley was the troublemaker. Bartley was the teenager who got in fights. Bartley was the one who rebelled against his cop stepfather.

Looking back, that's the one thing I regret. I could've tried to influence him. He would've done anything for me, but the truth is I *needed* him to draw their attention. I needed him to be the black sheep. That just made my wool whiter.

And it worked. I had put on the perfect costume. They believed me to be the golden child. They let me stay at Donna's house a full weekend, and over the summer, I went on a trip with her family to San Diego and the zoo and SeaWorld. Miguel and my mom never checked on me once. Donna's dad was a firefighter, and though cops and firefighters have notorious disdain for one another, they also share a first-responder respect, and so if I were with the Molinas, then it meant I was safe and secure.

I turned eighteen the summer before my senior year and told my parents I was spending the night at Donna's and maybe I'd just stay the whole weekend because her dad talked about taking us to Joshua Tree. I got a "Sounds good" and "Have a good time," but that was it. My brother stood in the doorway of my room while I put a bag together.

"What're you up to?" he asked.

I played innocent. "What?"

"Don't bullshit me, princess do-no-wrong. I know when something's up . . . and something's up."

I passed him on the way out. "You're paranoid, baby brother," was all I could give him. I felt terrible about that, but it was too dangerous to tell him anything, not this far into my plan, not when I'd waited this long. I was too close to the end and if my brother's trust was a casualty of my scheme, so be it.

I drove up the 5 from L.A. to Corcoran. It took about three hours before I started to freak, like an actor getting stage fright right as the lights come up on the first performance. I had looked up visiting policies, and if I made a request between the hours of two and four on Friday, then I could see him *if* he agreed to see me too. Now, so close to showtime, I didn't know if he would. He'd never written to me, I looked more and more like my mother, maybe he would deny the visit.

Finally, I arrived at the jail, and if you've ever been to a state prison, you know how terrifying the experience is. Prisons are designed to terrify you. Every bit of the process is intimidating. They don't need to have good customer service. What do they care if you come back or not?

But I went through everything, the ID, the fingerprinting, the metal detectors, the bag search, the mouth search, everything. They didn't strip me, but there was one guard who had a look in his eye that he might want to give it a try. I put on my scalded puppy dog look and they waved me into a room with what looks like a bunch of picnic tables, every piece of furniture screwed into the floor. I waited there with a bunch of wives and mothers and fidgety children for a good thirty minutes. I'm sure I was the only person between the ages of ten and fifty alone in that room.

After a half hour, a buzzer sounded and convicts entered and took a look around as though they were swimming up from underwater, and then my dad walked into the area. He looked beaten down, broken, like an old toy some kid had thrown in the closet and forgotten. He had gotten fatter, his cheeks were more like a basset hound's jowls, but when his eyes found mine, it was like someone had thrown him a life preserver. He lit up, crossed the room to me, and only at the last second caught himself before he scooped me up, something completely forbidden that would've cut off our visit right then.

We sat at our picnic table and he kept mumbling about how beautiful I was and asked me a million questions but wouldn't give me time to answer. I asked how come he didn't write to Bartley and me, and he looked at me like I'd knocked the air out of him. "I've been writing to you since the day they locked me up. Every week."

I wasn't surprised. The same suspicions that got me here held true for the lack of contact. I just didn't believe my mom when she insinuated our dad had sworn us off. He, however, was shocked. Shocked so much that I think whatever reluctance to tell me what he wished to tell me melted away. He didn't plan to spring it on me when this was the first time he'd seen me in ten years, but now, *now* all bets were off.

"Your mother and the cop set me up."

I must've sat there for a minute with a dull ache ringing in my ears, because the next thing I heard was the guard saying "Time's up."

My dad looked at me with alarm, stood, and before he walked back toward the guards, said, "I didn't knife your mother. They planned the whole thing. You have to believe me."

And I did.

—⁂—

"Now we're getting somewhere," I say.

Peyton swells and actually blushes. "Told you."

"You did. You did tell me."

She looks back at the house through the trees. The smoke has been going for a while now and Boone and the kids must be toasty. The sun breaks through the clouds and the combination of feeling the rays, seeing the smoke caterpillar out of the chimney, and Peyton's story warms me.

"Think we should head inside and check on things? Maybe finish this later?" she asks, smiling.

"Don't even think about it. Not when I'm just starting to like you."

"Oh, so that's how it is. Okay. Well, good to know the way to your heart is a good story."

"Always has been."

"Then when I'm done, you can tell me your story. Deal?"

"We'll see," I answer.

—⁂—

If I could plan for a year just to steal a visit with my convict father, then I wondered if I could put together something bigger, grander. My senior year, we read a book called *The Count of Monte Cristo*, and it opened my eyes. I don't think you're supposed to treat that book like a blueprint when you're eighteen years old, but maybe they should've thought about that before they made it required reading in high school.

I thought about going to law school and becoming one of those advocates for the wrongly imprisoned, but I'll be honest with you, Mr. Copeland, I didn't have the grades nor the patience. Maybe I could have gotten into junior college somewhere if the admissions department took pity on me, but law school was a mountain too high to climb. I'd tell you more about some other thoughts I had, but you already know I was a cop, so I'll quit dancing around it.

I graduated from high school and joined the LAPD. My mom blew a gasket, but Miguel talked her off the ledge and supported me all the way through the academy. The wood-cutter and the snake. A lot of people, when they hear that story, they identify with the woodcutter. But me? I like that snake. Stupid woodcutter dumb enough to warm up a frozen snake deserves to get fanged.

So I did the academy and I did two years in the sheriff's office like they make you do and when I got my assignment, I requested patrol in Miguel's district, and he was honored, and he made sure I got partnered with a friend of his, and the whole time I watched and waited. Before long I had a quick affair with a married lecturer.

He gave me the file on my dad's arrest in exchange for not calling his wife.

The report was straightforward. The arresting officer and only witness was Miguel Gutierrez, who reported he heard a scream while he was on his footbeat. There was an anomaly, however. Miguel responded to the cry for help alone.

I looked up who his patrol partner was at the time. A white guy, Danny Secott, two years on the job when the night in question happened, had only been with my stepfather a couple of weeks. He transferred to Hollywood Division and was driving a shop for the last five years when I tracked him down. We call patrol cars shops. It took me two or three Pink's hot dogs and a whole lot of whiskey one night, but I pried the story out of him at a bar called The Happy Ending on Sunset and La Brea between the hours of midnight and two in the morning. I guessed I knew what happened by this point so it was just a matter of Secott confirming and filling in the details.

He was partnered with Miguel that night and around 10 P.M., Miguel gets a call from a lady he's been shacking up with. Secott wasn't too clear regarding the details, but next thing he knows, Miguel tells him they need to walk over to Western and Melrose.

When they get there, Miguel sends Secott into a massage parlor where he knows the owner and wants to introduce them in case they have trouble. It's part of the new community policing initiative they got going now, he tells him. So he's inside there and realizes it's a barely legal whorehouse—I realize he's telling me this story in a bar called Happy Ending—and the Korean madame tries to unbuckle his belt, and all he can think of is that he's been set up. Is Internal Affairs about to bust down the door, are there cameras everywhere, is this why he's been partnered with Miguel Gutierrez? He'd heard of rookie cops fresh out of their sheriff's stint getting jammed up by Internal Affairs—they'd rather catch rookies who didn't already have pensions and friends and twenty years on the job. Rookies make easy IA prey.

Anyway, all these thoughts went through his head but none of it happened. He begged off from the Korean lady and whip-jacked out of there and searched the street for Miguel but there was no sign of him. Secott thought he was being hazed, this was all some kind of big joke, but no, no one was stepping out of the shadows, pointing fingers, and laughing, so he reversed course and walked up Melrose when his radio buzzed. Miguel was calling in a 245, assault with a deadly weapon, and the address was just a few blocks over.

He arrived in time to see a female victim with a gash across her head, a male assailant, knocked out, broken nose, and reeking of alcohol. Miguel, chest puffed out, said he happened to be passing by, heard screams, all that. He responded and knocked out the attacker.

Secott looked over the scene and saw about a million faults with the story.

"We got a problem, though," my stepfather says to Secott before he can voice his doubts. "Anyone asks, you're going to have to explain why you were in the rub and tug and I was three blocks over." Secott knew then that he had been set up, and so when Miguel wrote the report, Secott signed it, every word. He transferred after that, just had a queasy feeling about Miguel, because he knew the entire scene looked staged. Later, he found out Miguel married the victim, and it all clicked into place for him like the keyword in a codebook. He knew Miguel set a trap for the husband, but what could he do about it anyway?

When Secott finished telling me this story at two in the morning, he asked me what my interest was in all this anyway? Was I Miguel's new partner? No, I told him . . . I'm the daughter of the guy he arrested. Danny Secott spooked then and told me to keep his name out of any IA reports, and I told him not to worry about it, we never met. That was the last I saw of Secott. People think all cops in the LAPD know each other, but you could drive a shop one station over and I might never see you.

Anyway, I had no intention of bringing IA anywhere near this. In fact, I wanted them sniffing in any other direction than mine. Not for what I had planned. *The Count of Monte Cristo*, remember?

First, I worked a transfer for a convict named Lester Tomkins from Folsom to the Twin Towers under the false information he had a hearing with a trial judge regarding an appeal. It is surprisingly easy, or maybe not at all surprisingly easy, to forge transfer orders if you know the way the system works. I spent two solid years learning the ins and outs of the Los Angeles penal system, and the amount of money and resources that go to clerking errors is laughable. At least once a day, a prisoner from one jail or trial shows up in some part of the state he's not supposed to be in. Frustrated lawyers arrive to meet clients who are stuck in a holding cell five hours away. Judges suspend hearings because no one can seem to locate the accused. It was easy to put an order into the computer with one of the seventy clerks' chicken-scratch signatures on the paper copy and no one double-checking.

Lester Tomkins arrived in C-Wing, fourth floor, three days later, though he had no idea why he'd been transferred and no one to tell him the answer. The food was better than at Folsom, so he sure as hell wasn't going to complain. No. I know. I'll get to that in a moment. All will be made clear, Mr. Copeland. Stay with me.

The day after he gets there, I drive to the 9-1-1 call center and phone up the desk sergeant at the Wilshire Station, an old lifer I know named Jerry Massey who's half deaf and all the way dumb. I put on a voice and tell him I'm a kick out clerk at the Twin Towers and I need an officer Miguel Gutierrez to come over and sign some forms. I do this when I know it's the end of shift so that A. Jerry Massey will just put the orders through so he can go home; and B. Miguel is gonna jump all over the overtime. A solid C. is that he's gonna ditch his partner and come alone because the overtime orders don't extend to everyone.

After the call, I zipped over to the Twin Towers to see who I could see. I was still barely out of my assignment there, and most of the sheriff's officers in charge of the jail were guys I cut my teeth with and most of them liked me. I just needed one to do me a favor. Turned out I had my pick.

I chose this El Salvadoran kid named Luche because he once tried to put the moves on me and was easy to scare. Anyway, he owed me from the way his version of "putting the moves on me" was considered sexual assault in most states. The truth is I would've never been able to pull this off if I gave a shit about my job, but the uniform was always a means to an end for me, and this day was the end.

So my stepfather Miguel gets to the Twin Towers about an hour after his shift is over, and I meet him in the waiting area. He does a "surprised to see me" and I do the same, and I'm trying to keep the predator look off my face. As far as I know, I've already spooked him, but he gives no indication something's amiss.

This is the time to back out and quit, but I'll tell you the truth, it never crossed my mind.

He asks what I'm doing there and I say just visiting a friend from the academy, and he says he's there for some paperwork but he's not real sure what it's all about. I watch him talk to the desk sergeant, but it's clear no one has any idea about overtime or forms to sign and that's so normal, his suspicions aren't raised. He's a little pissed for driving downtown but he's planning on collecting that overtime regardless and *tick, tick, tick*, no sweat off his back.

I move to the desk and play innocent. I say that since he came all this way, I want to show him something. He asks what and I say it's a surprise and to follow me and Miguel checks his gun with the desk sergeant 'cause that's what you do and Luche buzzes us inside.

We go down a row of inmate cells to this little work area they got off C-Wing. Luche lets us in and shuts the door behind us.

Miguel has zero clue anything's up, but he's not stupid, so he's wondering what the surprise is. I sit at a workbench and gesture for him to do the same, across from me, so he does. "What'd you wanna show me?" he asks.

I drop my smile.

I can feel my eyes, my whole face going hard, and it's like I've already left the room. It's like I can hear my voice coming from my mouth but it's not in my ears. That's the only way I can describe it.

"Why are you looking at me like that?" he asks.

I say to him, "Miguel, do you remember a man named Lester Tomkins?"

Now it's time for Miguel to drop his smile. "What is this?"

"So you do remember him, that's good. You arrested Lester Tomkins five years ago, right? Arrested him with one hundred kilos of hash and 200 grand in cash, yeah? A huge bust for a uniform, one that got you a commendation and a temporary assignment to Narcotics.

"There was one problem though. Rumors started to go around that there were a lot more drugs and money in that stash house than were reported. Your partner, Edgemont? He retired and disappeared off the grid. Maybe when you divvied up your cut, he was smart enough to vamoose to South America, but you stayed here to grind because you had a new wife and new stepkids.

"Lester Tomkins squawked to everyone that he had a million in cash there, but it was his word against yours and Edgemont's, and that was never gonna work out too good for Lester Tomkins, was it? Plus you planted two guns that matched two unsolved homicides so Lester got life in prison instead of the ten to twenty he would've gotten for distribution. You made sure he went away for good. And because of the missing money, he got a severe beat down for a solid year in Folsom. All the time he's getting pummeled, he's seeing *your* face, thinking about what he's gonna do to you if he ever sees you again."

Miguel turns the color of brick and looks like he's going to explode. He leans forward . . . "Are you IA? Is that what this is? You ratting on your own father?"

"I'm not IA," I say in a steady voice. "And you're not my father."

"Now you listen here. This is fiction. This is bullshit. I don't know what you think you're—"

But I stop him with, "Who cut up my mother's face?"

It's the oldest trick in the interrogator's playbook, keep your opponent off-balance and hit him with a hook he never sees coming.

"What?" he stammers.

"I know you set up my father. I know he never raised a hand to my mother. I know you made sure your partner was compromised during the call. I know you were dating my mom while she was married to my dad. I know either you or she took that knife from his candy shop. The only thing I *don't* know is which one of you chopped her face to sell it. Did you do it or did she? Either way, it's sick. Either way, my dad isn't getting out of jail until he's an old man. I just wanna hear you have the balls to tell me. Whose idea was it? Hers or yours?"

"That's it," Miguel says and stands. "I've heard enough."

He charges to the door, but the handle is locked. Funny thing about jails is the doors only work from the outside. He turns toward me, his mouth pinched, furious. "What the fuck is this?"

"Let me try." I stand and slowly move toward the door. He steps out of the way so I can put my hand on the handle, but then I turn to him. "On the other side of this door is Lester Tomkins."

Miguel runs a dry tongue over his cracked lips. His eyes dart around. "What?"

"I had him transferred to this jail on a bogus FL-2. Right now, my sheriff's officer friend positioned him alone in the corridor, without restraints, armed only with the knowledge that officer Miguel Gutierrez—the man who cost him his life—is in here, unarmed. And when I knock like this . . . and I hit the door, *tap-ta-tap-tap-tap* . . . he'll unlock the door."

Miguel looks at the spot where I'm holding the handle, then back at my face. Sweat begins to trickle down his forehead.

"You're full of shit," he says, but he's not sure now.

I start to turn the door handle and he cries out, "Wait."

"Who cut her face, Miguel?"

"Come on now, Peyton. I looked after you."

"Who cut her face?!"

"I did!" he roars. "I did! But it was her idea, I swear it. Now what good is that gonna do you, huh?" His eyes roll like a rabid dog's. Saliva flies from his mouth. "Huh? What good is it gonna do you? You want me to go to jail? Your mom? Is that what you want? Because if I go down for this, then she——"

"No, Miguel, no," I say calmly. "That's not what I want. I want much, much worse."

And with that, I open the door.

———

She stops and grins. We stand at the path that leads to the house, about thirty yards from the front door.

"That's it?" I ask, though I know the answer.

"That's it."

"What happened to Miguel?"

"You can google it," she says, as a rental car crests the bend and pulls up the drive, Archie at the wheel.

"And your mother?"

"You know how police officers notify the relatives after a homicide? Since I was on the job, they told me first what happened to Miguel. Professional courtesy. I volunteered to pass the news on to my mother," Peyton says, seeing it. "My sergeant denied my request, said they had grief counselors for that, but I insisted. Said it was family and I could handle it. I don't remember if he agreed to my offer or just quit opposing it. The department had enough problems trying to figure out how to keep the press at bay regarding the murder of an LAPD officer in their jailhouse.

"So I went to my mother's house and told her the news. She didn't cry or ask more questions or run upstairs and shut her door. She just looked at me, stone-faced, like she foresaw this moment, me standing in her foyer telling her that her husband was dead."

"She suspected your involvement?"

"I left out any doubt. We fell out of contact after that."

"Where is she now?"

"A story for another time."

I nod and wave at Archie as he parks.

"All of what you said is true?"

"What do you think?"

"I think I need to access this side of you."

6

Boone and the kids eat lunch at the dining table with Peyton. Laughter rises and dissipates in waves, like screams from a distant roller coaster. I glimpse Peyton as she moves around the table to reach for a paper-towel roll. She says something funny as she pats the younger boy, Josh, on the head with the cardboard tube, and he squeaks laughter. Her face brims with mirth and mischief.

Archie catches me looking, doesn't say anything. We stand in the yard.

"What do you got?

"A start. I talked to a dude I trust and he said the job went through one of two fences in Los Angeles. A guy named Ezra Loeb or a cat named Wilson Wilson. You know them?"

I shake my head.

"Don't matter. I got you a couple of addresses should get you started. What's the word on sister love?" He tosses his head toward the dining room.

"I think she might be one of us."

"You figure that out while I was running around?"

"Call it a gut feeling. She might need some guidance, but she's got instincts."

"Hmmmm."

"It is what it is."

"I'll feel her out while you's in Los Angeles."

"What if the real hit man cometh?"

"You can't be in two places at once, so we'll just have to see. But you got a gut feeling about this girl . . . so what's the worst that could happen?"

He lights up a cigarette and shows his teeth.

I narrow my eyes and stuff my hands in my pockets.

"You look good," he comments, appraising me. "Healthy. No joke. Straight up."

"I know what you're doing."

"Ahhh, shit. Just take the compliment."

He squints and lets the smoke out so it can join the cloud ceiling above us.

—⁓—

I fly into Los Angeles the next morning, rent a car, and drive to a house next to the airport to pick up a bag of guns. If I can get to the correct fence from the two choices Archie gave me, maybe I can persuade him to call the hit back or give me the name of the contract killer so I can persuade him directly. Sometimes persuasion and killing are interchangeable.

It feels good to finally go on offense. During my time in Portland, I've been out of my element, off my game, like a racehorse who suddenly finds himself pulling a wagon. As I take a bag off a bed in the back room of this drop house in a quiet street in Long Beach, my senses awaken.

The bag is in the backseat of my rental sedan as I head up the 405 toward the San Fernando Valley, where Ezra Loeb works out of a building behind a paint store. According to Archie, he's been doing this work for thirty-plus years, surviving and thriving, so the most I can hope for is a meeting through proper channels. The middlemen, the fences, are in dangerous positions, standing between clients and killers, and as such, are vulnerable to information seekers like me. The ones who survive for decades know how to defend themselves, shore up their vulnerabilities.

I have respect for them, though respect does not grant them immunity.

I enter the foyer of the first address and am surprised by how corporate it seems: a lobby, a few chairs in a waiting area, a potted plant, and some prints of flowers on the walls. The only hint this is not an accounting firm or a law office is the giant man standing by the one door that grants access to the building's interior.

I approach him and ask to see Ezra Loeb. He observes me with disinterest, then talks into a headset. After a moment, he points at a camera and tells me to state my business.

"I'm here to consult with Ezra Loeb. I'm with Archibald Grant out of Chicago. I'm armed but I promise an armistice. I'm only here to make an offer and to have a few questions answered."

I turn to the beast by the door. "That's it."

His expression doesn't change.

"What now?"

"Have a seat," he says, and points toward the plastic chairs.

—⁓—

Thirty minutes pass, an hour. I'm an expert at waiting. So many people in this business like to play unnecessary head games, everyone looking for an edge, a power position, but I don't give them the pleasure. I don't check my phone, don't fold my legs, don't fidget. I don't rattle. I wait in the chair with an eye on the big man in front of the door. I'll give him credit, he doesn't twitch either, a pit bull poised for his next command.

Finally, he wands a fob over black glass next to the door, and it buzzes so he can open it. "Let's go, then," he says, his voice as big as he is.

I've interacted with quite a few fences over the years and they are as different as DNA strands. The smart ones, the top-shelf ones, maintain their positions by respecting the game, showing deference when appropriate, demanding it. They have systems in place for keeping their personal lives and professional lives separate. They know it's a career built on reputation, and the difference between respecting the job and disrespecting it is literally life and death.

We walk to a small room with a red door. I sit in the one chair and he leaves me there, locking the door on his way out. There is no other furniture in the room. A window lines one wall with a thin diamond pattern etched into the glass, bulletproof by the looks of it.

I don't have to wait long. A light illuminates the other room, and the glass I thought was opaque is actually transparent. I can make out a male figure on the opposite side, but he obscures himself in shadows.

His voice reaches me through a speaker.

"What can I do for you?" Loeb asks.

"I have no reason to hold cards close to my vest, so I'm just going to tell you straight, Ezra. Either you or a fence named Wilson Wilson accepted a contract on a businessman named Matthew Boone in Portland, Oregon, and assigned a hit man to kill him. I'm working for Mr. Boone, and I'm going to do what I can to keep him alive. I'm asking you to give me the name of your contract killer if you can't call him off."

I expect a long pause and receive one.

Finally, the metallic voice sounds through the speaker again. "What're you offering?"

"Your cut of the contract plus fifty percent."

Another pause.

"You want me to undercut my reputation for money?"

"I'm going to kill your man whether you turn me on to him or not. This is a courtesy visit because I have respect for you. You might as well profit from it."

The shape in the shadow shifts, the first movement from his side of the glass.

"You mentioned the other fence, Wilson Wilson."

"I did, yeah, but forget him. I already know the coin flipped in my favor and you got the contract. I can tell from this conversation."

Another pause, then, "Let me tell you about my counterpart, Wilson Wilson. He's bottom of the barrel. He's the gravel at the bottom of an aquarium, the green scuzz on the side. You need a razor to scrape it off the glass. That you thought the contract was awarded either to him or to me is an insult in and of itself. He's a blight on this profession, and he doesn't deserve to be in the same sentence with me. He's a back-alley pennies on the dollar hack."

"Sounds like you're the one wanting to make a proposal."

I hear him breathing now through the speakers, hot and labored.

"I want you to kill him for me. We have no ties, I don't know who you are other than you came from Archibald Grant out of Chicago, and that name carries weight. So you take out Wilson Wilson, and I'll give you the name of the contract killer assigned to hit Matthew Boone."

"No, thank you," I say politely and stand. "If you'll get your man to open the door, I can show myself out."

The light goes out in the other room and the window turns opaque again, a mirror. After a moment, the lock to the door in my room clanks, and I draw my Glock. I don't think they'll try to kill me on his property. That would be bad for business. Still, the giant man who showed me into this room might come through the door spoiling for a fight, and I'm not gonna let him get wound up.

When the door opens, though, it's not the big guy, but a squat, bearded man with eyes magnified by circle-lens glasses. He's dressed in a blue sweater and gray pants and his accent has a bit of an Israeli baritone, nothing like the scrambled voice that was coming through the speakers. He waves at my gun hand like I've picked up a paperweight off his desk. "Put that away, come on, now."

I stow my gun and hold up my hands.

"I show you my face. You seem like a serious man, and I want to show you I am serious too."

"I appreciate the gesture, but I'm not pulling a side job for you, Ezra. It's not out of disrespect. I can already tell you're an excellent fence. But I assume you've already sent out your hit man and the clock is ticking. I've seen the way you operate, so I'm going to assume the assassin you assigned to the job is all kinds of capable. I don't have time to settle a personal beef for you."

"This is a negotiation. I thought we were negotiating. You didn't let me finish my offer. If you eliminate Wilson Wilson for me, I will give you the name of the killer I assigned to the job, and I will give you the name of the *client*."

I was not expecting that, and he sees it on my face.

"Ahh, I've said the magic words, eh? If you agree to this, I'll give you everything you need to know . . . after I have confirmation of Wilson Wilson's death."

I toss it over in my mind. It would be a windfall to gain this knowledge, and he knows it.

"Do we have a deal my friend with no name?"

He extends his hand.

"Copeland," I say and shake it.

—⁂—

The dangling fruit is too tempting. My assignment is to protect Matthew Boone. If I have the name of the man who wants him dead, not just the killer but the client, I can eliminate the threat at its source. I can cut off the head of the snake. Eliminate the queen so she can't lay eggs.

My reservation is I have to trust a fence who gives away confidential information. I would be *earning* that information, yes, but Ezra Loeb would have to betray his own assassin plus the man who paid for it. Maybe he's setting me up, but I can't see the angle.

The way I die is from inertia.

The way I die is trusting the untrustworthy.

I was impressed by Ezra Loeb's operation, and showing me his face to cement the deal was a solid negotiating tactic, I have to admit. So why can't I see his play?

The address I have for Wilson Wilson puts him in a residence near downtown in a neighborhood called Eagle Rock. Blocks there have apartments, duplexes, single-family homes, home businesses, and commercial properties all on the same street. I am not sure which of these I'll encounter until I put eyes on the place.

I roll from the valley to downtown, avoiding the freeways and heading up Sunset. Traffic is packed and urban sprawl is everywhere. After the endless emptiness of Mackinac Island, the city is a shock to the senses. I'll take the sprawl over the snow.

It's jacket-weather cool here, and joggers in shorts and long-sleeve, body-hugging Under Armour tops dot the sidewalks. The absence of parking lots means cars line the curbs on both sides of the street, so it's easy to conduct surveillance from the privacy of one's automobile.

I find an empty ten feet of curb and parallel park against it, a half block up from the address Archie gave me. The building looks like a small home set up for moderate protection with bars on the windows and two tattooed, sleeveless-shirted Hispanics loitering on the porch. For outside eyes, it has all the markings of a drug house. That keeps the general public away. A few payments to the right DEA officers and LAPD lieutenants will keep the cops at bay, too.

A Mercedes S550 pulls to the curb, too much car for this neighborhood so it sticks out like a bloodstain on a white carpet. A man in a dark hoodie climbs out, the hood up, covering his head, so I can't get a good look. The two cholos on the porch rise and hold the door for him, and hoodie disappears inside with no familiar handshakes or embraces.

Wilson Wilson. Has to be. Only reason they would treat him with such deference is he's the boss.

A cavalier hit man would pounce once he spots his mark, but I didn't last this long being cavalier. This house could very well be fortified, so why deal with the two on the stoop plus who knows how many inside?

Experience tells me to follow the Mercedes and pop him when he's alone and defenseless.

Hours pass and the cholos are gone. They went into the house, walked out again, and headed up the street, away from me. One looked in my direction but took no particular notice of my car. If I thought he made me, I would've stormed the house without waiting to see what reinforcements he might summon.

Maybe I should make a move now, while the porch is unoccupied, while the watch shifts. Maybe I should stick to the plan and wait until he emerges and drives away.

The way I die is missing the details.

The way I die is overreacting to the details.

The way I die is lack of fucking confidence.

Wilson Wilson emerges from the house, hoodie up, and ducks into his Mercedes. The engine cranks and he guides his car up a hill. I mash the rental car's accelerator.

The way I die is impatience.

The Mercedes meanders right and left through Eagle Rock, avoiding highways, in no particular hurry. Through his rear glass, I see his head bobbing to some rhythm, the radio on, the bass thumping.

Wilson Squared waits too long at a stop sign and my spider-sense tingles—have I been spotted?—but a glow inside the Mercedes tells me he's wrapping up a text.

A few seconds more and he tosses on his blinker and turns West toward Hollywood. I keep a discreet distance and resurrect my tracking muscles. Always keep a few cars between your mark and you, never make sudden stops or jerks, turn away and double back if he drives erratically. The surveillance is easy, and he drives about three miles before he pulls to a curb and hops out to enter a guitar shop on Sunset. It looks like a warehouse, more mom-and-pop than corporate chain. The name on the sign says "Wilson Guitars," and I'm a little in awe of this dumb fuck. He's dabbling in retail musical-instrument sales while he runs a contract-killing business? No wonder Ezra Loeb felt insulted.

I hop out of the rental sedan and approach the store. There are a lot of cars on the street but not too much foot traffic. Los Angeles has never been a walking town. In the window of the shop, rows and rows of acoustic and electric guitars hang on peg hooks or rest in display stands, Fenders and Gibsons and Taylors and Epiphones. The glass is thick and reinforced with security gates that look like they slide up and down after business hours. COME IN AND START STRUMMING reads a sign. Christ.

A bell jingles when I slip through the front door.

There's a counter with a vintage register up at the front, unmanned. The interior is made up of tall shelves stuffed to the breaking point with amps, chords, pedals, strings, tuners, electronics, and every type of guitar made: basses, steels, Flying Vs, Strats, acoustics. Heavy rock music blares from somewhere in the back, and it takes me a moment to realize it's not a recording; someone is shredding a lead guitar in the bowels of the store. I can barely hear myself think, which means no one is going to hear me coming either.

I make my way down an aisle piled high with touring cases. Around the corner, I make out Wilson Wilson, his back to me, the source of the music, wailing away on a Fender, a solo from some rock song of his imagination. Maybe I'll let him finish before I pull my Glock and kill him.

He turns, mid E-string finger bend, and he's not Wilson Wilson, but an Asian teen who smiles at me with a "gotcha" in his eyes.

A small-caliber revolver presses against the back of my head.

"Kill the music," Wilson Wilson demands, and the Asian guitar aficionado deadens the strings with the palm of his hand. The sound of the solo stops, replaced by the low hum of the amp.

"Turn around," Wilson Wilson says.

A sharp contrast to Ezra Loeb, he looks like he belongs on the sands of Malibu Beach: blond hair, blue eyes, a vintage Quiet Riot T-shirt that looks ordered rather than collected. His eyes have a feature consistent with television preachers and cult leaders . . . the irises are completely surrounded by the white part, giving him a crazy affect.

The two cholos I last saw on the porch in Eagle Rock appear on my right and left wearing matching grins. They're so damned happy they pulled off a successful switcheroo, they're practically giddy.

Wilson Wilson keeps his .38 pointed at my face, those irises floating in milk.

"Okay, asshole. Who are you, who sent you, and why were you following me?" His voice has that Southern California lilt that makes me look forward to smashing him in the throat.

"Take it easy. I'm here because of Ezra Loeb. He wants a sit-down."

Wilson Wilson snorts. "Oh that is special. That is priceless. That prick wants to sit down with *me*, after he tried to run me out of town?"

He makes a noise with his throat and nose that might be a laugh but I'm not sure.

The cholos don't know whether or not they're supposed to join in, so they keep their eyes on me while making snickering sounds.

"Well, I got a message for him," Wilson says and starts to squeeze the trigger. I am not expecting our discussion to end so quickly but I recognize crazy eyes when I see them and I know he means to shoot me and send my body back to Loeb as a "Fuck you," but I've always been able to move faster than my enemies expect.

I mule kick backward, hard and lean, like a jumpy horse encountering a rattlesnake on the trail, and the force of my blow is delivered into the Asian guitarist's chest. He flies backward into the amp wall, and since he's still holding his Fender, the racket he makes is earsplitting, like a sudden thunderclap breaking over the top of you. The sound serves its purpose: disorientation.

I rocket forward and punch past the raised revolver into the throat of Wilson Wilson. A punch to the throat when you get your full weight behind it is the most devastating blow a dirty fighter can deal.

Wilson drops the gun without even squeezing off a shot. He staggers back, his hands clawing at his gullet as though trying to open a hole in his windpipe.

The cholo on my left is quick and might be into that MMA shit because he tries to duck under my arm and send an elbow to my jaw. His problem is all the practice with heavy bags and speed bags and grappling mats goes out the window when your opponent deals in death and doesn't play by the rules.

I dodge the elbow and drive my knee into his balls with everything I have. The effect is immediate. He doubles over, sputtering, his strength snapped, and my next knee connects with his nose, detonating it like a grenade.

The second cholo must figure whatever paycheck he's getting from Wilson Wilson is no longer sufficient. He breaks for the back door and is through it as though the building is on fire.

Wilson Wilson still has his hands to his throat but his eyes are on the revolver between us. It spins on the ground like a wheel of fortune. It points toward him, then me, then the cholo, then the Asian, circles through a second time, before it stops, pointed at him.

Prophetic.

—⚋—

On Larchmont Boulevard, in a neighborhood called Hancock Park, I find a bookstore named Chevalier's. It's small, comfortable, and crowded, with floor-to-ceiling shelves. It smells like dust and paper and knowledge and Risina. I met her in a bookstore in Rome when I wasn't ready for it, and she stopped in bookstores like this whenever we traveled to a new city.

I shouldn't continue doing things she did. I shouldn't revisit the past. I shouldn't stir up ghosts, smells, images. Risina in a bookstore, her legs curled under her bottom in a high-back chair, her nose buried in a Jeff Abbott thriller. Risina with Pooley in a bathtub, water spilling onto the floor. Risina staggering across a covered bridge, a knife buried in her side.

The way I die is overcome with grief and guilt.

A small woman named Liz with smiling eyes and a wily grin asks if I need help finding something and I leave with a book from Scandinavia.

There's a pizza place across the street that has New York–style giant wedges, so I wait for my slice to come out of the oven and turn my thoughts from the distant past to the immediate one.

Why did I agree so quickly to kill Wilson Wilson? Loeb barely got the proposal out of his mouth and I was running and gunning. To protect Matthew Boone, right? Or was I impatient to get back to spilling blood, taking lives?

There are two jackets hanging in a closet—one protector, one killer. Why was I so quick to shed one and don the other? Was it because one fit comfortably and the other fell apart the last time I wore it? And why the hell did Archie ask me to put it on again? He knows what happened the last time. He *knows*.

I am Copeland. I am Columbus.

Should I choose one name over the other?

Do I have to?

—᠁—

Loeb meets me in his office this time, his inner sanctum. His giant bodyguard stands watch in the room. He keeps his gun out and in one of his ham hock hands, but not pointed directly at me. Polite menace.

"You don't waste time," Ezra Loeb says, happy.

"No."

"What'd you say your name was?"

"Copeland."

"How come I don't know you, Copeland?"

"I don't like to be known."

"How is Archibald Grant?"

"Why?"

"You pleased with him?"

"He gets the job done."

Loeb leans back in his chair and his chin doubles. He looks at me like he's studying an experiment, waiting for the mouse to pick its way through the maze.

"Here's my offer. You move to the West Coast and you work with me. I'm the best fence in the United States, and I don't say that to brag. I say it because it's true. I'll take care of everything. Your housing, your weapons, your ammunition, your banking, your transportation. I will not miss a single detail. I have a feeling you're high-end, so I will give you high-end jobs. I handle all the research personally, and if you want to see one of my target files, I'll oblige. I'm not here to besmirch Archie Grant, but I'm telling you, you can do better. It's as simple as that. That's my pitch."

I nod, but only to let him know I mean no disrespect. "I appreciate the offer, Ezra, and I promise to carefully consider it."

"Good."

"But for now, I'm just going to ask for the name of the hit man and the client on the Matthew Boone job."

"Okay, yes. We had a deal and I will hold up my end of it, but I also want to explain why I made this offer. It is not my business to turn out my killers nor my clients, but these are special circumstances. First, they're both terrifying. I don't really have a second.

"The client is a Polish citizen named Piotr Malek. This is an evil man, the worst I've ever seen, and I surround myself with devils. It is up to you to decide how evil, and I will hand you his file so you may know what I know and you can see the kind of research I do. I took his money because I had no choice. I then assigned the kill to this man . . ." He hands me a second file. "Keith Watts. Watts has been in my stable for less than two years, and I made a big mistake taking him on. He's not a contract killer; he's psychotic. He kills the target and dozens of other people along the way. He once took out fourteen men and women on an office floor on the way to his mark. It was a massacre. I would've dismissed Watts, but I'm afraid of him, to be honest. I've been doing this job for thirty-five years and I have never been in this situation. When you walked in like manna from heaven, I thought, *I can kill three birds with one stone here. Take out my rival and get rid of these two demons, all in one fell swoop.*"

"Three birds, huh?"

"I'm scared of them. Bey, do I get scared?"

The big guy behind me grunts, "No, boss."

"See, I don't get scared. But this murderous bastard of a client and this homicidal maniac of a hit man have me jumping out of my skin. I feel for Matthew Boone, I really do, which may be why I didn't put together the greatest file for Keith Watts. I might've bought Boone some time."

"When did the assignment go out?"

"Six weeks ago."

"So he's in the strike window?"

"Yes. Eight weeks is usually it, but . . . yes."

"Okay," I stand, holding the files. "You've been fair. And I will consider your offer."

"Seventy-thirty. If we work together."

"Again, I'll think about it."

He stands, and we shake hands. Bey opens the door and shows me out. The files feel heavy and thick.

I am Copeland. I am Columbus.

Soon, I will have to choose which is stronger.

7

take a private jet out of Van Nuys so I don't have to switch out guns
and ammo when I get back to Portland. I'm alone, except for the pilots
and a flight attendant who brings me a plate of Chinese food from what
she assures is the best restaurant in Beverly Hills. I ask for privacy and
she disappears to the flight deck without being offended. I open Ezra
Loeb's first file and bend over a well-written, strong piece of research.

The man who ordered the hit on Matthew Boone, Piotr Malek, is
fifty-six. He grew up outside of Warsaw in a town called Wolomin.

His parents, like everyone else in Poland after World War II, were poor and stayed poor. Malek's youth is a mystery until he shows up at Moscow University in 1978. He earned a degree in chemical engineering followed by another in computer science. What he did in his primary education to garner enough notice to attend university in the Russian capital must've been remarkable. He graduated with distinction, then disappeared into the labyrinth of the Soviet government until 1989, when the wall fell, and he moved back to Poland.

He appears in various records after that—building permits and bank accounts and travel visas provide a timeline—but his longest employment stint was at Belchatow Power Station, which is unremarkable on its surface. A chemical engineer who ends up in the energy sector of his homeland seems a natural progression, though I don't profess to know the ins and outs of Polish politics. That he held his position throughout his country's volatile identity shifts speaks to either expertise or tenacity. That the power plant remains one of the most climate-damaging installations in the world is not Malek's fault and certainly can't be the source of Ezra Loeb's horror and spite. I don't take this fence for a radical environmentalist.

A few pages more and I get to the crux of it: Twenty-four plant workers died in an accident in 2004 at Belchatow. There was an inquiry. Malek held the title of Chief Engineer and some kind of fire spread on his watch and two dozen men perished. Malek was exonerated and the newspaper in Warsaw proclaimed the tragedy an "unfortunate accident." Official reports on the hearing went missing or were destroyed. Soon thereafter, Malek's bank account grew by millions. He left his position at the Belchatow plant and moved back to his nation's capital where he consulted with the Minister of National Defense. His position in the government remains unknown.

So what to make of all this? How do twenty-four deaths at a lignite-burning power plant result in a bribe and a defense post? How does that tie into a hit on Matthew Boone? And why was Loeb scared enough of his client to give him up to me? I feel like I've been given the answers to a crossword puzzle but the boxes don't fit the words.

I flip to the file on Watts, the hit man. It has more detail than I imagined it would be, mainly because shooters in my line of work tend to bury information about their history. Our pasts can be used against us, as I found out when a fence named Aiza sold my biography to a killer named Castillo. Many people died, including my wife, Risina, and the name Columbus.

"Keith Watts" appears to be his birth name. He was in and out of institutions since the age of twelve, including a two-year stint in juvie for torturing his neighbor, an eight-year-old girl. He hung her in her basement by throwing a rope over a chin-up bar, then released her to her feet long enough to catch her breath before he hoisted her up again. He was nearly beaten to death by the girl's father when the latter fortuitously discovered them. The girl survived and recovered. When the details emerged, prosecutors dropped charges on the father.

Watts did his time and then started killing for money, according to Loeb's file. He worked for a succession of fences in the South— Louisiana, Mississippi, Alabama—before he was busted for murder in Texas and did an eight-year piece at Huntsville. His release was either a clerical error or someone paid off the parole board; regardless, Watts lit out for the West Coast immediately. Loeb recruited him on the recommendation of a fence from New Orleans, but he thinks he was tricked into it. The New Orleans fence wanted Keith Watts off his hands and off his books and was only too happy to push him onto a colleague like a magician forcing a card. Since then, Watts performed half a dozen jobs for Ezra Loeb, all involving additional casualties to civilians, most involving criminal torture of the mark before he or she died.

Loeb is right. This man is a psychopath. I'm going to have to stop him before he makes his move, find him and eliminate him first, because his attack will most likely take out Peyton—and the boys.

His affinity for torture has me looking forward to it.

—⁂—

The safe house outside Portland is quiet.

No smoke rises from the chimney when I approach and I go on high alert, like a dog that hears a stick crack outside a window. I park quickly and leap from my car, but the front door is locked and inside the house, silence. The curtains are drawn, so I can't see through the windows, and unease sets inside me. I realize I don't have a key. I never asked for a key. Peyton had the key when I left, and Peyton's car is here but there's no sign of her or the Boone family.

I move around the house soundlessly, my ears up, my Glock out, and the wind picks up, the cold, remorseless Oregonian wind, and the hairs on my neck feel it, all of them erect and standing at attention. I thought I had time, but hit men never respect *your* clock, *your* schedule. They make their own time and exploit your sense of yours.

The windows on the side of the house are covered too, mocking, and the forest seems to have gown closer to the house, a trick of the shadows, the sun fading, falling. If I'm too late, if inside is mutilation and devastation, then the next job I perform will be free of charge.

A football thumps in the grass thirty feet in front of me, bounces, tumbles awkwardly, comes to rest. Josh leaps on top of it, then Liam on top of him, and they tumble, laughing, rolling over each other.

They stop when they see me with my gun up and freeze, their easy laughs dying in their throats. Peyton jumps around the corner, her pistol in her hand, but she catches sight of me and stops before she pulls the trigger.

"Oh," she says. "It's you."

—⁂—

I sit at the kitchen table with Boone and Peyton, empty soup bowls in front of us, tension in the air.

"So your recommendation is to stay here and do nothing?" Boone is restless. It's not his fault. It reminds me of Jean-Paul Sartre's story "The Wall." Mix terror, worry, and waiting, and the combination will drive any man to the brink.

"I'm going to find the hit man who took the contract and put him down. Then I'm going to find the man who hired *him* and make sure he hires no one else."

Peyton shifts her eyes from me to Boone to see how he's going to accept this strategy. He keeps his voice low to avoid the ears of eavesdropping children. "I have a business to run. A life to lead. They have school. How long do you think—" then he stops himself and squints his eyes tightly like all of this is too absurd. "I can't believe we're talking about this."

"Well, we have to talk about it because it's happening. If you want to live through the next month, then this is the way it has to be."

"You'll kill them?"

"Yes."

"This name you have."

"Piotr Malek."

"I don't know how I got on his radar. Or why. But can't we make him an offer . . . buy him out?"

"You'll be looking over your shoulder for the rest of your life, even if he agrees to terms now. You want to be sure?"

Boone nods.

"Then you unleash me."

Peyton might as well be at Wimbledon. Her eyes follow back and forth as we speak, enraptured.

"What did I do to him?"

"I don't know. Whatever it is, he thinks he's better off with you out of the way."

"Poland? He's Polish, you say. I've never done business with Poland. Or anywhere near there."

"Maybe Malek wants your company's software, and he thinks it'll be easier to acquire without you in charge."

"This goddamn technology. It wasn't supposed to be like this. It was supposed to help people, help governments, help law enforcement. What they want is a perversion."

He looks for approval from me, agreement, but the way things start out and what they become are rarely in the hands of the creator.

"How long?" he asks again, like a child accepting his punishment but haggling over the terms.

"I don't know. When I get to Watts, that'll buy us some time. You can check in with your office then. Do whatever you need to do business-wise."

"I should shut the company down. I don't need it. I've done enough."

"That's neither here nor there. It could make everything better or everything worse. I don't know why Piotr Malek wants you dead, but the whys don't change what is. Understand?"

He nods.

Peyton speaks up, her voice strong and confident. "What about me?"

"We'll talk later."

Boone rubs his hands up and down on the back of his neck, trying to relieve tension that won't go away. "You're asking me to tell you if it's okay to kill two men I don't know . . ."

"No, Mr. Boone, I'm not asking. That is what is going to happen. You have no culpability, morally or legally. It just is. What I am asking you to do is to continue to hide here, continue to have no contact with the outside world, especially your business, until I do my job."

"But I thought when I reached out to Curtis, I thought I was hiring a better bodyguard." His voice rises. "Someone to guard my body. Not someone who . . ." He stops, controls his volume. "Not someone who . . . who kills the . . ."

"You did. You did, and that's what I'm doing. There's a threat that isn't going away until I eliminate that threat. It's no different than if you had cancer and you hired surgeons to cut it out before it spreads."

He stares at me a long time, trying to wrap his mind around this new reality, seeing if my logic is acceptable.

Finally, he nods. "A cancer."

"That's it."

"I . . . uh . . . I should go check on Liam and Josh."

"Okay."

He stumbles away, sleepwalking.

Peyton takes a bite of an apple.

"Cancer?" she says, and a little juice dribbles onto her chin. "That was a good one."

—◊—

The house has an outdoor fire pit on the side with a view of the driveway, so we turn on the gas and set if aflame, and Peyton and I sit while the logs crackle and throw out just enough heat to keep us comfortable. A light is on upstairs in the boys' room, and we can hear Boone reading to his sons, even though they're too old for bedtime stories.

I had plans to read to my son—I wasn't going to do it like all the parents before me. I wasn't going to read the Magic Treehouse and the Hardy Boys and the Elmo books. I was going to read him *Lord of the Flies* and *Of Mice and Men* and *The Old Man and the Sea*, because those authors wrote about the way real people acted, real boys talked, real life was lived. That was my plan until real life was lived and he's not my son anymore. I wonder what Jake is reading to him now.

The way I die is curiosity.

Peyton puts her hands near the fire to warm them.

"What about you, Mr. Copeland? I told you my deep, dark secrets . . . you got one for me?"

I shrug, lost in my past. "There's nothing to tell. I just do my job."

"Horseshit," she says. "You're no more bodyguard than Kermit the Frog. And you're not, nor have you ever been, law enforcement. I can spot a cop a mile away, and you've never carried a badge."

"What am I then?"

"I'm guessing some kind of special forces. Some kind of army intelligence we never hear about that does shit in countries we're not supposed to be in. How close am I?"

"All over it," I give her.

She accepts it reluctantly.

"While you're gone, I want you to know, I will not let them out of my sight. I don't need much sleep. When I catch a few winks, it'll be inside their room, next to the locked door. I will stick to the Boone family like Velcro."

"Keep doing what I need to do until it is done."

"Glad to. These boys—these boys, they're something special. The dad I don't know about. I want to like him because it's my job to keep him alive and I want him to be worthy of it, you know, but he's sort of closed off, which I can't really blame him for, knowing what's going on, there being a price on his head and all.

"But the boys, Josh and Liam, they're great. They get along more like friends than brothers, and they're so sweet, asking me how I'm doing. Maybe I shouldn't care. I don't know. But it makes me happy to stay here."

She bites her lower lip, like she's been talking too much and she's gonna stop now.

"I had an old boss once who explained to me that when I did a job, an assignment, I had to make a connection with my mark so I could sever the connection."

"Mark? What do you—" then she stops herself. "Oh." It comes clear to her. "Ohhhh. Okay. Go on." She settles back in her chair, her cheeks flush.

"He said it was a mental game you play so you can continue to do the job effectively. Find something terrible in the person you have to put down, latch on to *that*, breathe *that*, so when it comes time to dispose of it, it's like cutting out the rotten part of an apple."

"Does that work?"

"I think so. I don't know. I've never had a hard time sleeping at night, I know that. But maybe, maybe on this side of the coin, maybe the protection game is similar. Maybe you have to find something to love about your client, breathe *that*, so you'll do anything to save him. Or them."

Peyton snorts.

"What?"

"I'm sorry. But you sure aren't doing anything like that with Matthew Boone and his kids. You barely look at them."

"Yeah, well." I toss a stick in the fire. "Maybe that's for you and not for me."

I'm up early, doing sit-ups and push-ups, when Josh enters the room and sits on the bed, watching me. I ignore him, hope he gets bored and leaves, but he sits on the bed with owl eyes, his legs dangling above the floor.

"What?"

"Just sitting," he answers.

"Sit somewhere else."

He stands, moves over a couple of inches, and sits back down again. I continue with my sit-ups.

"Are we going to go back to school?"

"You're taking a break."

"What about homework?"

"No homework."

"What about science fair?"

"No science fair."

"Can't Dad email Ms. Hoang and find out what we have to do, and we can work on it from here?"

"No."

"Why not?"

"Because."

"Because why?"

I stop, mid sit-up. "Are you a kid?"

"Yeah."

"Are you a lawyer?"

"No."

"Then quit asking me questions and just accept what I say."

"You're funny," he says.

"No, trust me, I'm not."

"Even *that's* funny," he says and giggles.

I go back to the sit-ups.

He slides down on the floor, hooks his feet under the bed, and tries to keep up with me.

His father pokes his head inside the door. "Josh. What's up?"

"Exercising," Josh grunts as he struggles to get his elbows to his knees.

"Come on out of there and don't bother Mr. Copeland."

Josh does one more sit-up and then hops up and claps his hands together. "I did ten," he says.

"Nine," I say without breaking my rhythm.

"Maybe it was nine," he says to his father as he takes his hand and walks out of the room.

—m—

Archie arrives at ten the next morning with his best commodity: information. We stand in the foyer. He has his fedora in his hands, and I hold a file he put together on Watts. "This is it?"

"All I could get on short notice. I mean, it's a lot of backstory Loeb already gave you, but there's a little more detail in there. The problem is we don't know when he got into Portland, where he's flopping, what he's driving, whether he got his guns here or brought them with him."

"What *do* you have?"

Archie sneers at me, shakes his head. "I was trying to find a junction point, but I ain't got one."

"I can't sit and wait."

"He ain't gonna find this place."

"I'm not insulting you Archie, I'm just saying if we play defense, we could be here a long time, and the longer we sit, the weaker our defense gets. It's just the way it is."

"So whatchoo thinking, Copeland."

"A mistake."

"What d'you mean a mistake?"

"I mean we need Boone to make a mistake and I put down Watts when he comes."

Archie's eyes light up, seeing it. "I feel you," he says. "The problem is . . . if Watts is as reckless as reported, he's liable to take a whole bunch of people with him biting on our trap, right? You know I'm right."

"So we keep it as controlled as possible."

Archie moves his head from side to side like he's a judge's scale settling on the balance. "Control the chaos, huh."

"If we can."

"That's never worked out too well in our favor when we tried it before."

"Doesn't mean we stop trying."

Archie spreads his lips into a smile, his teeth catching the light, twinkling.

"What?" I ask.

"There he is," he says, and shakes out a Camel.

—m—

We can't go back to the car wash, Archie tells me. He heard chatter cops are sniffing around the joint so the owner closed up shop, declared "maintenance problems," and took a trip to Florida.

Archie calls Curtis, who calls a guy, and Peyton and I go out to meet him.

We're at a rest stop near the Oregon-California border, watching for a truck to go by so we can follow it to a private location. Rest stops are good for making contact but not the best place to conduct business. State patrols check them regularly and if you linger too long, you're bound to drum up suspicion. We stopped and got some tacos from a gas station store, those things looking more and more like mini-malls these days.

Peyton attacks a burrito. "This surprises me," she says between bites. "I didn't figure you for a fast-food guy. I mean, this stuff goes right to my ass, but it's just so good. I've seen you eat since we started, just coffee and garbage, and you still look like . . ." she gestures at me.

"Genetics," I say, although I met my father and that hypothesis doesn't hold.

"Must be," Peyton says. "Your ticker or your metabolism or whatever it is they call it must be just going *tick-tick-tick-tick-tick* all the time. It's not like that for me, let me tell you. First, the things I like to eat are . . ."

A semitruck with a trailer rolls by and blasts twice on its horn as it switches lanes.

"There's our ride," I say, and Peyton and I hop off the picnic table and climb into my sedan. We follow the truck for a couple of miles. The side reads "Rainbow Party Rentals" and on the back are "How's My Driving?" and "This Vehicle Makes Wide Right Turns" signs. There aren't many cars on the highway and I haven't seen a police cruiser since we left Portland.

The truck's turn signal blinks and we follow without making it too noticeable. He turns right down a country lane, and we wait five minutes and follow. "Keep your eyes peeled," I tell Peyton.

"For what?"

"You'll know."

A few miles of a winding, wooded road and I think maybe I missed it but then Peyton says "*There*," and I see where she's looking. The front grille and bumper of the semi poke out from behind a burned-out, abandoned remnant of a farm equipment sales office. I ease the rental into the gravel lot and swing around behind the building so I'm parallel to the truck, blocked from any eyes on the road.

A bearded man with half-moon crescent eyes sits on the back bumper of the rig, smoking a cigarette and swiping his finger on an iPad. He stands as we park and approach.

"Okay," he says. "Curtis tells me you need some gear."

"She does," I say, and nod at Peyton.

He opens a door cut into the big bay doors on the back of the truck and helps her onto the bumper and inside. I follow, and the man enters behind us.

Phosphorescent lights come on like we're inside a store, which is more or less where we stand. "Okay, look, everything we have is custom made but generally modeled after a brand you've heard of. What're y'all looking for? Tac gear? Ammunition? Rifles, revolvers, semiautomatics, fully automatics?"

As he continues, the lights flicker and brighten, illuminating the trailer until we see an impressive arsenal of weapons and gear. Each wall is covered floor to ceiling with drawers, pegboards, clothing racks, and shelves like we're inside a Walmart.

The salesman has an impressive Southern accent, drawing out his vowels as he runs down the equipment. "Okay, so what we got here is a Kevlar tactical bulletproof concealable security vest. That's got one and a quarter pound of areal density. Real nice. That's full coverage. Look at that. Front, back, both sides. It's got trauma plate pockets with a self-suspending ballistic system. You like it, I'll throw in a tactical response helmet with a polystyrene liner and three-millimeter polycarbonate face shield. Maybe you need it, maybe you don't. Someone's firing at your head . . . yeah, you're gonna need it. There's top of the line and this is above that."

Peyton fingers the gear, squints at me. "This is nicer than anything we had at the LAPD."

"You're right about that, sister. No tax money's paying for what we got."

He continues down the center, gesturing to his left and right. "Up there we got our version of the Arsenal Strike One. It's got a seventeen-round detachable magazine and a nice short recoil. Fit your hand like a glove. Ours is like Coca-Cola, even better than the real thing, you ask me.

"Okay, maybe you want something with more bite. Here's our take on a Sig P227. That's a .45 caliber. It's gonna hold seven plus one and will put a hole through anything you need to air out. You want more than that, I can put you on a sprayer, but you look like you're concerned with precision rather than suppression. Am I right? You don't gotta answer. I know I'm right. Go with the Strike One."

Thirty minutes later, Peyton is the owner of brand-new body armor minus the helmet and two handguns, one semiauto and a revolver she can keep in her boot. We take a knife belt too and no money exchanges hands because Archie and Curtis have an understanding.

The Southern salesman closes the back doors, locks them up, tips his cap our way, and I'm expecting a "Pleasure doing business with y'all," but he gives us an "Okie, dokie, pokie" instead, hops into the cab of his semi, fires it up, and rolls out of there.

Peyton helps me load the new purchases into the rental sedan.

"Okay," she says as she shuts the trunk. "Just who the fuck are you?"

—⁂—

We eat bagel dogs from a food truck parked in a vacant lot between little houses east of downtown Portland. There's a propane heater next to a picnic table so we take seats and dig in. "I kept saying, damn, this guy must be CIA or some other alphabet but it didn't really work with the way you carry yourself. I've never met a contract killer before so I just don't . . . I didn't know."

"Hmm."

"How long?"

"A long time."

"How many?"

"A lot."

"You ever get caught?"

"No."

"How do you even start in something like that?"

"Just like this."

"What's that mean?"

"Someone who did the job talked to me the way I'm talking to you."

"Oh." She puts down her bagel dog. "Ohhhh. Oh, no. Sorry, man. If that's what you're thinking . . . that ain't me."

"Okay," I say.

She picks up her food again, puts it back down. "That's just not me. What I told you before, about what happened to Miguel. That was a one-time deal. That was a personal thing."

"Okay," I repeat. My bagel dog is almost gone. I don't know what they add to the bread, but it's delicious. The food trucks in the Pacific Northwest know what they're doing. I stand and toss the paper tray into a trashcan and head back toward the car. "Let's go."

Peyton hasn't moved, her eyes far away. What she's seeing—the future or the past—I have no idea.

"Hey," I snap, and her eyes drift to me. "I said, 'Let's go.'"

She gets up and follows me to the car, dazed.

She leaves her wrapper and Coke can on the table, forgotten.

—⚋—

The trick is to give away Boone's whereabouts without making it too obvious we're setting a trap. Knowing Keith Watts's penchant for casualties, it would be best to lead him somewhere isolated. Innocents are innocent, and I'm not in the business of killing people who aren't in the game. It's not moral . . . it's practical. Each person who dies has friends and family members who want answers. Once, a bystander in Paris was run over as a direct result of my actions and his brother turned out to be a crime lord who put a price on my head. It got messy from there. Lesson very much learned.

Upstairs, I knock on Boone's door and he answers with a frown, his face drawn, like the events of the past month have aged him years. I pull out a drop phone and hold it out to him.

He looks at me, wary, like I'm offering a poisonous snake.

"Who do you trust at your company?"

"Uh, my CFO, Donald Blake. My head of IT, Jessica Chen."

"Who don't you trust?"

"I don't know."

"Think."

"Louis Newman, head of sales. Big gossip. Always in everyone else's department, telling them how they should do their jobs. I should've axed him a long time ago but I put it off."

"Call him. Tell him for reasons you can't explain, you had to duck out for a bit. And you need him to meet you in Forest Park at the hiking trailhead at 9 p.m. Make up something he needs to bring to you, a laptop, a file, whatever sounds plausible."

"Okay. Is this bait? Like you're baiting the killer?"

"That's right."

"Why do you think he'll go for it?"

"I'm guessing that Piotr Malek has someone in your company feeding him information. If it's not Louis Newman, it's someone else, but he'll hear about it and blab."

"How do you know?"

"It's what I would've done. If I can't find the target, I find someone the target is in contact with and go through him."

Boone shifts uncomfortably, then takes the phone from my hand. He tries to do it quickly so I won't see his hand shaking.

"When this is done, you can keep that phone and check in on your business for real. But let me eliminate this threat and buy enough time to remove future threats completely."

He nods, nods some more. "I'll call him right now."

—⁂—

Archie drops me a mile away, and armed with a trail map, I swing into the park and hike to find the best view of the parking lot. I wear a brown and green hoodie with brown pants that might as well be camouflage in the forest. I can't believe how green the park is this time of year, but a light dusting of rain just as the sky darkens provides me with the answer. I'll take the green over the endless whiteness of Michigan anyday.

No stars tonight, no moon, and though the parking area is surrounded by an equestrian village, a nature center, and a couple of bathrooms, dense forest presses in on it like a shroud. I timed my arrival with Boone making his call, so Watts can't beat me to the lot if he takes the bait.

Cars come and go in fits and starts, like the rain, but no one suspicious emerges.

A couple of hand-holding hikers, a teenager on his mountain bike, a group of parents and children here to ride horses enter and exit the lot. They park, they move out, they return, they drive away, and as the park closes, the lot empties. I hole up in a thick copse on the top of a hill with plenty of cover, and I'm seated, low to the ground, with no trail nearby, opposite the equestrian center. Someone could flank me, but it'd be impossible to know I'm here with my back to a tree trunk. My watch reads ten till nine.

Archie will drive into the lot at five after. If another car is here, he's to park along the far side of the area, flash his lights, and see what reaction he gets. He's in the vulnerable position of this plan, but he insisted on taking it.

Twin cones of light sweep the forest and a Buick rolls into the parking lot slowly, like a child entering an unfamiliar room. The car is nice, one of the luxury series, befitting the head of sales of a multimillion-dollar company. It circles the small parking area a couple of times, and when its headlights bounce off the restrooms and illuminate its own windshield, I make out a single driver, no one else in the car. He's got a full head of hair but that's all I can see before the headlights cycle past like a prison spotlight and the windshield darkens again. The car circles into a U-turn and backs into a spot. Dammit, I can't tell if it's Watts driving the Buick or if it's what's-his-name the head of sales. The car cuts its engine, then its lights, and faces the entrance to the parking area like a dragon in a cave.

I steal a glance at my watch. Five past nine.

The engine of the Buick *tink, tink, tinks* as it cools. My ears perk up and I'm watching for movement in the forest around me in case Watts has the same idea I had, my eyes long since adjusted to the dark. Nothing. No animals twitching, no owls hooting, just a dark heaviness above the treetops that seems to close down like the lid of a coffin.

Archie's SUV eases into the lot and stays on the north end, away from me, per the plan. If Watts makes a move, I can slip in behind him and put him down. Pop, pop, and take him out before he knows he was set up.

Archie parks thirty yards away from the Buick and points his headlamps directly at it, so the driver has to shield his eyes with his forearm. It is an amateur's gesture, the gracelessness of it, and it makes me think this is the head of sales after all, running the errand Boone assigned him.

Archie flashes his high beams twice, and the man in the Buick leans over to the passenger seat, then opens the door on his side and climbs out holding what looks like a laptop, but it's hard to tell. He keeps his eyes shielded with his forearm as he takes a hesitant step toward the SUV. His build is soft, not that that means anything. I've seen contract killers in all shapes and sizes.

"What the hell, Matthew?" he calls out, and I'm convinced this is the guy Boone called, and maybe I was wrong, maybe this prick didn't blab to anyone, maybe he's innocent. We set the trap but the fox never crept into the henhouse. And if that's the case, then Watts has a different plan of attack or isn't as good as I thought.

Head of Sales continues across the lot like a moth pulled to a candle, clearly holding a small computer and not any type of weapon, clearly not the guy we are hoping for, when a new set of headlights wash over the lot.

A park ranger's truck, a giant four-by-four, green, with Park Service printed on the side in reflective yellow letters crawls into the area like a shark in a lagoon. It has one of those side-mounted spotlights, and it illuminates Archie's window and then splashes Head of Sales so he's lit up from both sides. I don't know what this ranger usually breaks up in a state park right before closing time but I can't imagine this looks good. The ranger opens his door to step down from the driver's side of his truck, and when he does, the side-mounted spotlight swings with the door. The light cuts across the Buick's windshield, and I catch movement inside the car that wasn't there before.

A second man in the back seat, head hunched, watching.

Watts is here after all.

The ranger is built like an ox, has to be pushing six foot five, and his movements are slow, a tired guy at the end of a tiring shift just trying to get his shift done, but he has to deal with whatever vagrants are left in the park.

"Park's closing," he speaks in a weary voice that says he'd rather talk to otters and bears than humans.

Head of Sales looks like he has no idea what he's supposed to do next. He throws a look over his shoulder at his Buick as if to say "What now?" and the back door whips open, and I hope Archie sees it too, but I'm not waiting. I break from my cover and fly downhill toward the lot, moving ungainly but moving, moving over uneven ground, soft ground, moving over roots and brush and rocks and this ambush plan isn't much of an ambush if I can't reach my target before he starts shooting.

He does, two shots rip through the night, light followed by sound, lightning then thunder, and the ranger cries out and drops. Head of Sales crumples, his head pitches forward and then whiplashes back because of the tendons in his neck.

Archie has been in a firefight before. He punches the accelerator and his SUV jolts and bolts, like a racehorse bounding out of the starting gate. Another two shots ring out and spider his windshield, and Archie's SUV lurches right and bounces over Head of Sales's corpse before it crashes into the side of the restrooms.

The ranger screams from where he crumpled to the ground, much louder and higher pitched than two minutes ago, a higher register, and whatever Watts's bullet did to him took the bass out of his radio.

Watts hasn't spotted me and he hurries toward Archie's SUV, all playing out in front of me as I descend the hill, avoiding trees, trying to keep my feet, and the hood of Archie's SUV is accordion smashed like a Frank Geary building, smoke billowing from it and the driver's door opens and Archie stumbles out.

If he's been shot, I don't know. If he's wounded, I don't know. None of it will matter in mere moments, endless seconds, as Watts crouch-steps toward him like a soldier attacking. And he's quick, quicker than I would have believed, and I'm not going to get there in time.

Archie stands up straight and Watts sees he's not Matthew Boone, he's a thin black man instead of a stocky white man, and it is in that moment, that second of confusion, hesitation, that stops Watts mid-charge and he rises from his crouch and lowers his weapon as his body catches up to his mind and I reach him.

He doesn't have time to process he's been duped before I put two in the back of his head.

He nose-dives forward and momentum sends his body bouncing across the parking lot. It finally stops, limbs like noodles swirled in a bowl, and his body stills.

Archie's eyes move from Keith Watts's corpse to my face.

"You used to be quicker," he says.

—※—

"Where'd he get you?"

I drive the Buick across the bridge back toward downtown where we can drop it.

Archie scoffs, digging into his shoulder. "He missed. This is glass from the windshield." He pulls out a piece the size of a pebble, holds it up in the light, his fingertips bloody, then rolls down the window and tosses it out over the bridge. "That asshole targeted the ranger and the other dude before he shot at me. You see that shit?"

"I saw it. He's a psychopath."

"Well he's a dead psychopath now."

We left the ranger in the lot, passed out, after keying his radio to an SOS signal so someone will come looking for him.

The Buick keys we found in the pocket of the no-longer-aptly-named Head of Sales.

"This should buy us at least a week. I mean, Loeb ain't gonna rush back to his client and tell him the hit failed, so most likely, this cat in Poland thinks all systems go."

I nod, hold the wheel steady.

"What?"

"Nothing."

"No, you got a look about you. What?"

"It just seemed easy."

"My shoulder begs to differ."

"I mean aside from Smokey Bear driving into the lot, it went according to plan."

"That's why it's called a plan."

"I guess."

"Then *what*?"

"Nothing. You're right."

"Shiiiiiiit. Now you got me unsettled."

We drop the car in a Safeway parking lot, and I run into the pharmacy for some Neosporin, gauze, and Band-Aids.

A quick field dressing, and we find a bus heading to the suburbs, then steal a car out of a Walmart Supercenter by the Columbia River. Another twenty miles and as we near the safe house, a Suburban passes in the opposite direction, two people inside, and there is something familiar about the driver, though he has his hat pulled low. I don't get a good look at him, and maybe that feeling I had is spreading like a disease because Archie seems fidgety, too.

Smoke pours from the chimney as we round the bend and the safe house enters our view. It is still and quiet.

Dread overwhelms me, the virus attacking the host.

The way I die is infection.

8

Misery loves company, yes, but that implies misery either passively gravitates toward those who are already miserable or it attracts misery to it like a fishing lure winking below pond scum. The question is: Does misery *cause* company, whether subconsciously or willfully? Do miserable people want everyone around them to be just as miserable and so set about to author that misery?

Why did I leave that drop phone with Matthew Boone? Why didn't I hold on to it until *after* I was sure the threat was neutralized?

Why did I hand it to him with the power on so that any hit man with a modicum of skill could ping it as soon as the incoming call was answered? Why did I assume Watts was working alone? While we were drawing Watts out, was he drawing us away from his mark?

Did I want Boone to suffer as I had suffered?

Does Archie see it on my face now?

The door is locked, but this time I have a key and I bust through it to find Peyton unconscious on the floor, two holes in her outer-wear but breathing. I flip her over so she can take more air into her lungs, unbutton her shirt, and work my fingers to where her freshly purchased body armor stopped the rounds. A bottle of water pours its contents on the wooden floor nearby. Peyton's eyes open, flutter, and then focus on me. "Oh God," she manages.

"When?"

"I don't know. I heard a noise, stepped to the door thinking it was you, and then gunshots . . . I don't remember."

"Boys! Matthew?" I yell, but there is no answer.

Archie leaps up the stairs like a panther up a tree, faster than I thought he could move, but after a few seconds, yells out, "Nothing."

"They were . . . they were in the backyard. I came in to get some water . . . oh, God," she repeats, pissed.

I don't have to help her to her feet. Peyton, Archie, and I spill into the backyard, calling out "Boys! Boys! Boone!" in tandem.

I'm thinking about the Suburban we passed and I quickstep through the short grass and head into the woods, pulling out a click-able flashlight. Peyton and Archie follow, spreading out, fanning out like a volunteer cordon after a child goes missing. Peyton cups her hands to her mouth, "Liam! Josh!"

The woods are a different kind of dark, an all-encompassing black-ness except for the small area my beam penetrates.

I see a shape sprawled on the ground, animal-like, and it's the size of Matthew Boone, and it's wearing what he was wearing when we left, and I wasn't here to protect him, but as we approach, he bends his knees, his body inch-worms up, and he's alive. His hands are bound behind him so he can't pull his face from the dirty leaves, and I dash to his side and roll him over onto his ribs and then I slit the white cord that lashes his wrists together and pull the gag from his mouth and he is free.

"The boys," he croaks, and points deeper into the woods, and I've heard that voice before, I understand that voice, because I've worn his shoes, I know what it's like to lose a boy in the woods, and I'm not sure if I caused this in some way my conscious mind can't imagine.

You're miserable, you're miserable, you're miserable, you're miserable my footsteps tell me as I crash through the woods in the direction he points.

The safe house recedes until it is only woods surrounding me now, 360 degrees of branches and trunks and leaves and pine needles, and then I hear a new groan in the brush, ten feet to my right, buried in the dirt where I would've missed it except for that sound, that grunt, that plaintive moan, just to my right.

I spin the flashlight in that direction, and I spy a tangle of clothing and dirt and branches and it's the older boy, Liam. He turns his face to the light and blood pours south from a gash in his cheek and he cries out now, his lungs bursting, and all around me Peyton, Archie, and Matthew Boone erupt through the woods and then Boone is on the ground next to his son, pulling him up to his chest, searching his face in the light from my beam, blanketing him with "My boy, my boy, my boy."

Liam wails and cries, "Josh! They took Josh."

—⁂—

A blanket, soup, and some of Archie's Neosporin and Liam is distraught but okay. The story comes out from the three of them: Two men in black masks who knew what they were doing; they eliminated the threat from Peyton first, shot her in the chest, and left her for dead.

Next, they went after Boone and the kids. When Boone saw the muzzle flashes inside the house, he yelled to the boys to run, and instinctively they all dashed for the woods. Next thing Boone felt was something like a brick to the back of his head and they had him tied and gagged and left him there. He thought he was going to die then, but for an unknown reason they left him behind and stalked smaller prey. Liam heard steps behind him and spun in time to see a flashlight arcing toward his face and then he was on the ground, too tired to move, and that's the last thing he remembers before the sound of my voice calling his name.

"Did you see them take Josh?" his dad asks, looking for some hope to cling to, but Liam shakes his head. He didn't see anything after the flashlight cracked his face.

"Okay, it's okay," his dad says, mouth drawn.

"Are we going to call the police?" Liam asks his dad but looks at me.

"Let us talk in the other room," I say, and nod the adults toward the door.

"It's not your fault, Liam, none of this is your fault," Boone offers his son, but there's no comfort in it.

The untended fire in the living room has died, reduced to a few embers glowing an angry orange.

Boone speaks in a heated whisper. "Liam's right. We have to bring in the cops now."

"And tell them what? You hired a hit man to kill a guy in the park?"

"He's dead?"

"That's right."

"Then who—who were . . ."

"I don't know."

"You don't know ANYTHING!" he bellows.

Archie steps between us, "Okay, okay, settle down."

Archie dead-eyes me like I'm the one who escalated things. He pushes me back a few steps, gently but firmly.

Peyton speaks up, "It's my fault. I shouldn't have come inside."

No one answers her, no admonishment but no assuagement either.

Boone collapses into a leather chair, buries his face in his hands. "Why didn't they kill me when they had the chance?"

"I'm going to find that out."

"How do we get him back? How do we get Josh back?" He lifts his head and his cheeks are tear-stained.

"I'm sticking with the original plan. I'm going to find Piotr Malek, the man who put the price on your head, get him to tell me where your son is, then end him and end all of this."

"You're leaving? My son is *gone!*"

"The person who took Josh is working for Piotr Malek. He's alive and will stay alive until Malek gets what he wants from you. Now we can sit here and wait for your phone to ring and hear what that is or I can be on a plane to Europe finding the shot caller."

"How will you find him?"

"He'll find him," Archie inserts.

Boone's shoulders slump like the burden of holding back the dam has broken him. He tries to talk but starts sobbing, tries again, breaks again. Liam appears in the doorway, his eyes swollen and blotted, and he breaks for his old man until they are in each other's arms and I have to turn away. I'm not sure if it's because of shame or jealousy.

Peyton walks to the kitchen, hugging her arms against her chest, tormented.

—✽—

Once more, I meet in Loeb's office in the San Fernando Valley. He's relieved to hear about Watts's demise. He's been checking the Portland news and saw an item about a double homicide in a state park along with an injured ranger who was hazy on the details but glad to be alive. Loeb thought either Watts or me or both of us were dead in that lot, and he decided to wait to see who showed up on his doorstep. He's relieved it's me, or he's good at pretending. I explain that Malek had an alternate plan, one where he hired someone to kidnap Boone's son while I was preoccupied with taking out his assassin. Loeb takes this information stoically, like he's a doctor listening to a patient's chest.

Finally, he raises his eyebrows. "Well that's disconcerting," he says without sounding disconcerted. "It means he went around me."

"Like he didn't trust you."

Loeb leans back. I can see him making calculations, accepting conclusions, discarding others.

"I don't know who else Malek might've hired. Tandem jobs can be . . ."

"Disconcerting?"

He looks up to see if I'm mocking him, but my expression is blank.

"Yes. But I'll make a promise to you," he says in his frog's croak. "You can ask around about my promises. I did not put a second man on this job. I would've told you. Piotr Malek went around me."

"How's he gonna feel when he finds out his alternate approach was successful and your man is dead?"

Loeb fidgets in his chair. His hands nip at a loose thread on his knee, a piece of invisible fuzz.

"I imagine he's not going to be happy with you," I continue. "I imagine whatever deposit he made to you, he's gonna feel like he was ripped off. I imagine Piotr Malek won't like that feeling."

"What're you suggesting?"

"That we both have a problem. I have to go to Poland now, find Piotr Malek, put a gun in his mouth, and pull the trigger. Any way I slice it, that's going to take some time. Just flying there and back is going to eat up days. If I get lucky, I have him in a week, but all I have is your file and that's background, not a kill file. So I have to do my own reconnaissance, and that's time, time, time. Something Matthew Boone's son doesn't have. It's my experience kidnappers hold their victims long enough to get what they want with no intention of giving them back alive. That kid is getting dumped whether I kill Piotr Malek or not."

"He might be dead already."

"Might, but he was taken and not left dead in the woods. Malek wants something from Boone and maybe he'll use the kid to lead him by the nose or maybe he wants a straight-up swap. I don't care. What I do care about is getting that kid back alive at the same time I get to Malek since I can't be in two places at once."

"I'm not—"

"I'm going to ask you to put your considerable experience into finding out who he hired for the tandem job. I want you to treat it like your life depends on it. However you need to do that, you do it, and you feed the name to Archie Grant, at this number."

I slide him a slip of paper. "You do that, I'll be in your debt. I take that seriously. You don't, well, seems like you'll be piling up enemies, and that's not a good career move."

Loeb's eyes shift to the door.

"Call out for Bey," I say calmly. "See what happens."

Loeb picks at his pant leg, but the loose fuzz is gone. In a very low voice, he whispers, "Are you threatening me?"

"I am the definition of a threat."

"I looked you up," he says. "I talked to people who know Archie Grant. And they don't know you, Copeland. Someone, somewhere must've heard of you."

I lean back and keep his eyes clamped to mine. "Maybe you should consider why they don't."

I abruptly stand and Loeb winces. He's a man used to having control over people, and losing that control has made him jumpy.

"Archie will update me with your progress."

"What if the boy is dead? You can't blame me. I've cooperated fully. You wouldn't be this far without me. You have to admit that."

"Just get me the name."

"London."

"What?"

"Piotr Malek. He's not in Poland. He's in London. He lives in Clifton Villas. That's all I know. I don't have an address. I was going to tell you, but I . . . I'm telling you now."

I take a step toward him but stop myself. Instead, I nod, turn, and go.

Loeb is either going to do what I ask and help Archie, or he's going to burn down this office and never look back.

Either way, I plan to see him again.

—⚯—

I take a flight from LAX to London, first class, with the seats that adjust all the way horizontal. I can't carry weapons but that's all right, there's a scrounger named Olmstead I've used who can get his hands on anything. I hired him in Paris to back up a sewer line and flush a gangster from his home. He procured a van, hazmat suits, bags of manure, and weapons, all within a day.

An hour after takeoff, I pull my hoodie over my head, turn the chair into a bed, and sleep.

Heathrow is a mess, as always, masses churning around elevators and coffee klatches and duty-free shops like pilgrims at the Wailing

Wall. Without my guns, I feel like an amputee. My hand moves to my hip, the small of my back, my ribs, searching for my missing limb, and returns to my pocket, unsatisfied. It's rare I'm this vulnerable.

I negotiate the maze and hit the queue for the black cabs and am on my way to Hyde Park to rectify that feeling.

Olmstead's office is under an ambiguously named, disreputable looking "repair shop" that encourages few customers. An older man with a scowl dismisses me when I enter.

"Got to turn you away, son, too busy," he mumbles without looking up from a laptop.

I say Olmstead's name and he closes the computer, a different man, and guides me to a stairwell hidden behind a rolling file cabinet. "Down you go," he says, and waits.

I glide down the stone stairwell, a claustrophobia-sufferer's nightmare, the steps steep, both walls brushing my shoulders. I hear the file cabinet roll back in place behind me like a mausoleum stone, but it would be hard to turn and see it. How long has this hidden room been down here, 400, 500 years?

A couple of corkscrew turns and I'm at the bottom where a pair of bulbs hanging from strings illuminate a musty basement with an arched ceiling and walls lined with wooden shelves. A few tables and desks occupy the center of the room and a space heater glows in the corner.

Olmstead, tall, bald-headed, with black-framed glasses I remember from the Paris job, stands and approaches, warm but all business.

"Heard you were dead," he says in his working-class accent.

"I am," I respond.

"Aye. Copeland it is then? That's what Mr. Grant says."

"That's right."

"What can I do for you, Mr. Copeland?"

"Guns to start. Couple of Glocks. Extra rounds."

"Holsters, then?"

"I got 'em. They're empty though."

"Aye. Copy that."

"Clothes. Winter gear. Middle class."

"Copy."

He makes notes with a stub of a pencil on a snatch of paper, the back of what looks like a cleaning bill.

I move over to a row of shelves. This must be what a prop master's truck looks like, rows and rows of disparate items that served a purpose one time or another and might be pressed into service again. A London officer's uniform, a blonde wig, road construction signs, another sign written in Arabic, a pair of walkie-talkies, stacks of casino chips, a stuffed-animal unicorn, a bathrobe from a hotel in Paris—remnants from past jobs.

Olmstead's an expert at finding whatever a contract killer needs to complete his job, from counterfeit money to forged artwork to perfect replicas of uniforms, IDs, licenses, badges. The little pieces of a plan that gets an assassin through a door, past a guard, into a hallway, invisible, undetected, free to make his kill and escape. His collection is like a museum of deception, and since Olmstead never knows when he'll be called upon, he keeps a healthy inventory of items he is sure will be needed—hospital gear like syringes and stethoscopes, police uniforms from all over Europe, UN badges, Interpol badges, business cards with made-up names and phony phone numbers. He also deals in weapons and ammunition, a one-stop shop for all contract killer needs. He's kept this business thriving by his ingenuity and his dedication. He's the best scrounger in the world, as far as I'm concerned.

"You need a uniform then? 44 regular if I remember correctly."

"I don't know yet."

"Reconnaissance then?"

"Not even to that stage I'm afraid. Just trying to locate the target."

"No file?"

"This one came up suddenly."

"I see. It's an instant gratification world, innit? All hurry, hurry these days."

"You're right about that."

"Well, I'm here when you need me. Once the plan's together, call and I'll find what you need."

"You ever come across the name Piotr Malek? Polish national. Energy mogul."

Olmstead scrunches up his face, deepening the wrinkles on his forehead. "Can't say I have. Your target?'

I nod.

"Haven't heard of him, but that's not saying much. I don't get out on that side of the fence too often."

I nod, not even sure why I brought it up. He's a scrounger but he doesn't scrounge information. When he mentioned the file, my lack of background on the mark became glaring.

"I just thought . . . I wasn't thinking."

"What else then, Mr. Copeland?"

"I will phone when I . . . when I narrow my options."

"Very well. Give me a minute here and I'll get these things. I have some of them here. The rest I'll bring to your hotel."

"The Savoy."

"Nice. Very well."

He moves off, reaching to a shelf here, a drawer there, the layout of the place disorganized to anyone but him.

—m—

I check into a comfortable suite at the Savoy, and Olmstead shows up within an hour with a dozen hanging bags of clothes and several shoe boxes. When he finishes, he stops at the doorway, takes off his Donegal cap, and rubs his bald scalp.

"You said you're lacking a file and you got a little time pressure, so I put in the pocket of that coat there the name of a man in London I trust. He deals in information. Mention my name and he'll be at your service. Might help you with the pace of this, though I'm sure you're capable either way."

"I appreciate it."

"Very well then," and he's out the door.

—∞—

I met Olmstead's man, first name Marcus, no last name, two days ago in the lobby of the Savoy and now we're to meet on the steps of the statue at Trafalgar Square. He's a quirky little bastard, a round man with caterpillar eyebrows and a red nose that speaks of many nights of many pints at many pubs. I have no idea if he's effective—Archie hadn't heard of him—but Archie vouched again for Olmstead, and if Olmstead vouched for Marcus, then . . .

I asked Archie if Loeb had called or if he had made any contact with the kidnappers. The answer was none. None from Piotr Malek, none from the two men in black masks, none from anyone.

Questions start to prick at me like an itch between the shoulder blades. Where are the goddamn demands? Why didn't the kidnapper shoot Boone in the chest when he had the chance? What are they waiting for?

The way I die is ignoring the itch.

The way I die is moving too fast.

The way I die is putting trust in the wrong people.

The way I die is out in the open, without answers, answerless, useless, used up, a failure, ignorant, alone, forgotten, never remembered, wasted, a waste.

Trafalgar Square is quiet and cold. A few stragglers loiter, tourists taking selfies with their phones, but most Londoners bustle through without looking at the fountain, their collars pulled up, scarves wound tightly around their necks, earbuds blocking out the world, eyes never leaving the sidewalk except when they come to a street crossing, gazing a few feet in front of them but distant, not seeing at all. The dead-eyed vision of the modern pedestrian. Bad for civilization but great for those of us who don't want to be seen.

Marcus heads toward me, his body moving as though there's a Hula-Hoop in perpetual motion around his middle. He has much too bright of an expression for people in our profession, which is alarming rather than reassuring.

"Got it, got it!" he announces while still twenty meters away, holding a manila envelope, nearly mowing down a bundled jogger headed in the opposite direction. "Beg your pardon," he calls out, but the jogger only stutters and keeps going.

Marcus reaches me and takes my arm. "Let's keep moving, that's how I like to do it, keep walking, keep the CCTV cameras guessing and Orwell's corpse spinning and all is right with the world."

We stroll toward the National Gallery and he keeps his voice low like he's just remembered his fair share of cloak and dagger movies. The manila folder is tucked under his arm like a football.

"So your man Piotr Malek does not live in Clifton Villas as you were told. He does own a home there, understand these are not flats, oh no, heh heh heh, these are homes, quite posh. He owns one as I say, which might be why you were misled, but it is his sister Gosia who lives there with her, ahem, wife."

We turn past the gallery and move up Charing Cross Road, dotted with mild traffic as we swing around the National Portrait Gallery.

"So Poland then?"

"Ah-ah, not so fast. I said his sister lives in Clifton Villas. Piotr Malek lives outside London in Maidenhead in a mansion fit for a king. Do you know Cliveden House?"

I shake my head.

"No, no, of course not. You're a Yank. Ever watch *Downton Abbey*?"

I shake again.

"Quite good actually. Quite good. Well, Cliveden House was owned by Nancy Astor. It was the meeting place of political intellectuals who were called the Cliveden Set, anyway, huff huff, never mind any of that, what you need to know is it's a hotel now, and the house Piotr Malek bought two years ago practically sits in its shadow. You can book a room there while you do what it is you need to do. Just a suggestion. Your decision, my good mate, your decision."

We step left onto Irving Street where traffic is lighter and make our way toward a small park. The sign at the gate announces Leicester Square Garden. A marble fountain is in the center, a statue of Leicester I presume atop it, but the water is shut off this time of year.

Marcus arrives at a bench, sits down clumsily, and pats the seat next to him.

"Come on, rest a moment, won't hurt, won't hurt."

I join him. The red bloom on his nose has spread to his cheeks and is spotty, like vines dotted with flowers.

"Do you smoke?" he asks, expecting my head shake. When he gets it, he raises his hand, "No, no, of course you don't. Mind if I do?" but he's already produced a cigar and a flame touches the end of it. "Ahh, that's it. Nasty habit but it has its moments." He expels a jet of smoke from the corner of his mouth. "So this house owned by Piotr Malek is set back from the road, four floors, eleven bedrooms, fourteen baths, indoor swimming pool, elevator, two-level garage, set on 500 acres.

"He employs two full shifts of bodyguards, ten separate soldiers, who work staggered weeklies. I don't mean to suggest that one team goes on and one team goes off. They stagger the individual soldiers so every team member on both shifts works with everyone else. I refer to them as soldiers because all of Malek's bodyguards are Wojska Specjalne. I have no idea if I'm pronouncing that correctly . . ." He pats me on the knee. "Polish Special Forces, you see. All out of Krakow, all together since 2007. They are paid very well, their families are taken care of back in Poland, they are loyal to the death."

"Maids, housekeepers, cooks?"

Marcus lights up and his whole body shakes. He pops up quickly, like a jack-in-the-box hitting the last notes of "Pop Goes the Weasel."

"Keep moving, let's keep moving in case any . . ." and he taps his ears, points at a seemingly harmless construction crew. "Yes, the staff as it were. I like the way you think. So there are about two dozen regular employees, some Polish, some English, one West Indie. They're listed in the file but I haven't been able in the time allotted . . . I haven't been able to sniff out the weak links. If you find one, that may be the best way to make the chain snap. Yes, ha ha, roff!" He mimes breaking a chain.

"That said, I have an alternative idea in there I would like to bring to your attention."

He waits for me to say something but I don't see the question. I ask, "What's that?" and satisfied, he points in the air as though he's a politician making an election-rattling point.

"Right, well, Piotr Malek has an English tutor!"

His face jiggles as he puffs on his cigar. His mirth is infectious. I'm amused by ol' Marcus. He likes his job, that's easy to see, and I've been surrounded by so much darkness, it's nice every now and then to stand next to a light.

"Yes, yes, we have a *My Fair Lady* situation here in reverse. Enter Madeleine Graybill from Cambridge University, a maiden fair and free, one hundred pounds of lean English tenderloin, hm, hm, hm," and then the dam breaks and great rolling laughter bursts from Marcus in disaster-movie proportions. It's a symphony of laughter, all orchestra sections at full volume. I let the flood trickle to a leak, until he finally regains control.

"Yes, well, so, as you will see in the file, I think the tutor might be shagging her client, your mark, and I think she might be your skeleton key, but all I can do is present the case. It is up to you to make the decision. At least that's how we do it on this side of the pond."

"The same."

"Good, then . . ." he makes a silly bow, complete with a finger twirl, and hands over his file. "If you should need anything else, Mr. Olmstead knows how to ring me."

Marcus takes off one glove and thrusts his hand in my direction. I do the same and we shake. He heartily pumps my hand, everything about him exaggerated, and turns and waddles back toward where we entered the park.

I put back on my glove, look down at the manila envelope, stuffed and bulging, and spy a bakery outside the gates of the park.

My stomach grumbles.

—⁜—

Madeleine Graybill has red hair and a vanilla face. She's Scottish, not English, it seems, and inherited some of her homeland's roughness in her cheeks and eyes. Not pretty, plain.

I follow her into a coffee shop where she orders an espresso and sits at a table by herself with a paperback copy of *All the Light We Cannot See.*

A book lover, and my mind flits to Risina's face, and then the image dissipates as quickly as it appeared. It happens often. I'll hear an expression or see the back of a head or some sign on the highway or it's the way a girl is laughing in an advertisement, and for a second, Risina floats right in front of me. Here's this Scottish woman who looks nothing like my dead wife, but the way Madeleine's eyes dance over the words in her book summons Risina from the grave.

Do I want these flashes to disappear, go away completely, or am I seeking them, seeing them even when there's no reminder?

Her espresso arrives and she flashes the server a smile, and the warmth that rises over the roughness in her eyes gives me pause.

She sits for thirty minutes, her legs crossed. Every now and then she reaches for her espresso cup and sips, her pinky extended. She puts the book down at one point, makes a face as if she's shocked by what she's reading, then picks it back up, and Risina flashes in front of me once more. I've seen that identical behavior before, the surprise of the story forcing her to put the book down for a moment and acknowledge the shock, then the call of reading on too overwhelming to ignore.

A few minutes more and Madeleine marks her place in the book, stands, and dons her coat. I rise at the same time, beat her to the door, and exit in front of her. Instead of letting the door swing back into her face, I hold it politely, and she shines her warm eyes on me.

"Thank you," she says.

"*Nie ma za co*," I answer.

She stops abruptly as though I shocked her with electricity.

"You speak Polish!" she remarks, her eyes dancing.

"No," I say and smile. "A little, I guess."

—⁂—

We walk up St. Martin's Lane and then right on New Row toward Covent Garden. "You're kidding me," I say after she tells me she's a

Polish translator and teaches English as a second language to a few Polish nationals.

"I have no idea what possessed me to say 'You're welcome' in Polish when you thanked me for holding the door. It was like a bird whispered in my ear."

She looks at me with naive innocence, as though there is no deception in the world, that I said a bird whispered it in my ear and coincidence and fortuitousness are just as natural as the air we breathe. Bless her.

"How did you come to know a little Polish?" she asks.

"I spent a year in Warsaw," I confess, though six weeks on separate occasions is closer to the truth. Once to kill a priest who played brinkmanship with the wrong city official, and a second time to get information out of a newspaper reporter who worked for the Associated Press and was covering an upsurge of U.S. troops in the country. He had been reluctant to talk to me but was persuaded with a double shot of carrots and sticks. I hope Madeleine is more forthcoming.

The market carts are out, even in February when the sky is clear, and Madeleine stops to browse multicolored soaps in the shapes of eggs.

"I forgot to ask your name," she says.

"Jack Walker." It's a name I've used many times because it invites no further questions and slips easily from memory.

"I'm Madeleine," she reciprocates.

"Well, it was very nice meeting you, Madeleine." I take a few steps away, then stop like I just had another thought. "You mentioned teaching. Maybe I could get your card and inquire about learning more Polish."

She cocks her head at me. "Is this a pick-up now?"

I affect a blush, and she breaks into laughter. "I'm taking the piss out of you." She reaches her hand out, and adds, "Give me your phone."

I hand her the phone Olmstead supplied and she taps her number into my contacts list.

"How do I know you're not giving me a fake number?"

"Tap it and find out."

I smile, nod a good day, and head away. I don't turn to see if her eyes follow me.

—···—

I don't have the normal amount of time I'd like for a kill. I can feel an invisible countdown clock hovering over my head, ticking toward doomsday, restless, hungry.

The kidnappers will make their move within a week, their own clocks ticking, antsy. Probabilities suggest they've already killed the kid, but nothing sits right about any of this. So why am I not following Madeleine back to her flat, moving this along faster and further? Why am I in London? Why did my plan of attack involve moving far from Peyton, far from Matthew Boone, far from Liam? Why are all connections severed? Why are all emotions suppressed? What does it mean to live without contact?

The way I die is my insides ripped out, my heart dangling from a hook in front of my face.

There is some information I need to plan my next move. Loeb hinted at it back in Los Angeles, and whenever I've made a kill in the past, I've always tried to internalize the evil of my mark so when I eliminate him or her, it's like I eliminate that part of me. It allows me to kill again, psychologically. This job eats you, even if you follow the rules. The way to keep the hellhounds at bay is to truly hate the mark you are assigned to put in the ground. I hate Piotr Malek for taking a boy instead of killing his father. That's low work, base. It reveals the character of an amoral man.

It could be enough, but Loeb said he was evil before the kidnapping. His report mentioned the deaths of twenty-four people at a power plant in 2004, after which Piotr Malek became a rich man. So what's the rest of that story?

A few google clicks and I stand in the lobby of *The London Times*, asking to speak to a reporter named Jeremy Doyle. The receptionist makes a call and twenty minutes later, a frumpy man who looks like he sleeps in his clothes appears from behind a glass door.

"Hello. Gina said you're with Hodder & Stoughton?"

I shake his hand.

"Yes, an in-house imprint called Textile. It's a play on text and tiles, you know like they . . . never mind. I keep telling Randall it's too much to explain."

The reporter examines me like I'm some kind of alien creature.

"Anyway, sorry, I'm nervous. Is there some place we can talk?"

"Yeah, yeah, of course."

He shepherds me beyond the glass.

Print reporters are a dying breed in the world of personal blogs and instant tweeting. If you dangle a book deal in front of one of them, they'll tell you everything you want to know.

"Did you read *Voices from Chernobyl* by Alexievich?"

Doyle nods. "She won the Nobel."

"That's right. I worked with her when I was at Norton. I came across the articles you wrote about the Belchatow Power Station accident back in 2004."

"I was stationed in Krakow then. Just happened to be around when it all went down." His eyes twinkle.

"It was a long time ago," I say, dipping my hook in the water, shining a light on the tasty bait.

"Not too long. I remember it like it was yesterday."

"Do you think there's a book there?"

He leans forward and blows out a snort of air. "Oh, yeah, without a doubt."

"I don't know. I mean at its core it's a pretty standard power plant accident, nothing remarkable about it, right?"

"Okay, let me stop you right there. What'd you say your name was?"

"Walker. Jack Walker."

"Let me stop you right there, Mr. Walker. This *isn't* a standard story. No way. I mean that's the cover story the Polish government used, yes, sure. That's the *reported* story. Hell, I reported it." He smooths out some hair on the top of his head, actually licks his palm and pats it down.

"What's the *real* story? I'll be honest, I heard some whispering. That's why I'm here."

"You were testing me, huh?"

"I just thought it sounded a little far-fetched. Government conspiracy shit."

I'm guessing but it seems a fair guess based on Loeb's report. Jeremy takes the bait.

"Okay, here's what I heard firsthand from two people who worked there. You want the short version or the long version?"

Before I can answer, he says, "Short version is the head of the power plant purposely murdered twenty-four people, but you already guessed that one. The long version is where it gets interesting. You got time?"

"Nothing but."

"Good, good, because if I write this for you, it's gonna be a best seller."

"Let's hear it then."

A couple of stray hairs stick up on his head like antenna and he pats them down again.

"Okay, here goes . . ."

—〰—

The Belchatow Power Station covers about 4,000 acres and has twin 300-meter chimneys that spew exhaust into the dead center of Poland to the tune of 30 million metric tons of carbon dioxide per year. This place is sprawling, smelly, nasty, and this is fifteen years ago, before regulations and carbon capture technology and all that. The coal from the plant comes from a giant strip mine nearby, so there's just a layer of nastiness covering the whole operation. Now, the guy overseeing all of it is a very smart, very ambitious man named Piotr Malek. P-i-o-t-r but pronounced Peter.

So you know, here's who I'm talking to when I did the reporting. I'm talking to the operations manager. I'm talking to a security official named Gorski who is "No longer with us" and yes, those finger quotes are intentional. "No longer with us." I'm talking to several menial laborers who worked there for several years.

So I do some digging and I learn Malek went to school in Moscow. Okay, yes, he was in Moscow but he wasn't in school. He was GRU inside Russian intelligence, and his contemporaries there are a murderer's row of Russian agents—Naryshkin, Lunev, Trofimoff, some say Putin himself. Okay, so he does a decade in Moscow in foreign intelligence. A lot of where he went and who he went with and what he was doing is spotty, but I have some ideas. Bosnia. Kosovo. Qatar. This guy was in every hot spot and everywhere he went, people died.

Okay, regardless, he returns to Poland, and he rises quickly in the energy department, all his orders coming straight from the Kremlin, I suspect, and this traitor to his nation gets rich and climbs to the head of the Department of Energy, which becomes the Polish Power Grid Company in '97. He rides the wave from public to private without ever wiping out.

Okay, stay with me. This is where it gets . . . insane. 2004.

Okay, there's an accident in building 6 between the pulverizer and the boiler. In the official report, two dozen workers were called in to clean out a faulty conveyor that carries crushed coal from the pulverizer to the boiler. I can draw you a diagram if you want. Pulverizer's here, boiler's here, conveyor belt runs between. And here's where the questions begin. I'm a reporter and I live for questions.

One, why do you need two dozen bodies to do what could be accomplished by ten? I'm getting this from the head of operations and maintenance, whom Malek conveniently sent home that day. Operations, security, safety, and management heads were all sent home with no explanation. Why, right? Now, granted, none of them would talk to me on the record. Three wouldn't talk to me at all, but operations . . . Piotek, Piontek, something like that, I'll have to check my notes. He was rattled, but I slid him a stack of bills and some vodka and he opened up like a tin can. He said he'd deny it if I reported anything, but I still have my notes. Anyway, so question one is why are there two dozen people doing a job ten could do?

Question two is why were all two dozen workers *political prisoners*?

His eyes glow and he leans back, licking his lips, and those two stray hairs stand on his head again like soldiers snapping salutes. He ignores them and his face wiggles up and down like a bobblehead doll.

"This was not a state factory making license plates where prisoners are routinely brought in to do manual labor. This is a one-time affair, a first and a last, two buses filled with prisoners brought in on *that* day, to do *that* job.

"Okay, so I start drilling down on these prisoners and let me tell you, it wasn't easy. The number of the dead was widely reported, but the names, the families, who actually died, that was always being *sorted*, as internal investigations went on indefinitely.

"Still, I worked my way inside and checked prison transfer records and prison populations and one domino led to the next and I realized these weren't state prisoners, these were *dissidents*, all of them. Some were Chechen rebels who had escaped to Poland and were picked up on dubious charges. Others were Ukrainian nationals, some were Poles, some Russian, but there were twenty-four people who had either spoken out against the PiS party, which was rising to power in 2004, or the Kremlin.

"So here's Piotr Malek, right, who grew up in the shadow of a Nazi prison camp in Krakow, marching twenty-four political enemies into a power plant and roasting them alive. Hitler's proclivities not far from his mind, I can assure you."

He shakes his head at the wonder of it all. "How's that for a book, eh? It's got a bad guy who is Hitler-adjacent, it's got innocent victims, it's politically charged, I mean, tell me, what am I missing?"

I shake my head. "Why didn't you report this before?"

"Scared, maybe. Too much work. Worried I'd get to the end and it wouldn't add up. Worried I'd get sued. This is a bad time for reporters, you understand. I don't know. I'm a coward I guess."

"Why would you write it now?" Irrelevant to what I need—I've already gotten everything I hoped for—but I genuinely want to know.

"For the advance, right?" He smiles big and claps his hands together. Then he points a finger at me. "Kidding, mate, kidding. No, in all seriousness, I think enough time has passed and maybe people who were reluctant to talk would talk now. Like Chernobyl."

I nod. "Okay, look, you've been very helpful. Do you have a lit agent?"

"No, I mean, I've spoken to a few . . ."

"No matter. Give me a few weeks to pitch this proposal upstairs. I'm sure I can get it through, just a formality, but I gotta do it."

"No, yeah, of course."

"Once I get the sign-off, I'll send you the names of some lit agents. Or if you want to find one on your own . . ."

"Okay, yeah, no, fine."

"Great."

I stand and Doyle enthusiastically shakes my hand, nearly jerking it off my wrist. What is it with these Brits and their handshakes? Dollar signs and Nobel prizes sparkle in his eyes. "This is wonderful, really. So unexpected."

"Don't celebrate yet," I admonish. "And do me a favor and don't mention this to anyone. If Hodder catches wind you're shopping this, they'll just back off completely. We've been burned before and they say they won't play that game again."

"Oh, yeah, no. You came to me. You get first shot, Mr. Walker."

"I'll call you as soon as I hear."

"Thank you."

I get to the door of the conference room and turn the handle. Before I exit, I turn back to him. "Twenty-four political prisoners burned alive."

"Like Auschwitz," he says, and shakes his head in wonder.

9

You're not going to like me when this is over. Any goodwill I've earned by telling you my story over this last decade is about to evaporate. You'll ask why I would hurt an innocent woman. You'll say there could've been other ways, safer ways, where the innocent were left out of it. But you've forgotten who I am. You'll say I didn't take the time to plan another route to Malek and you are right. I won't deny it. I'm a killer and I hurt people to get to my target, sometimes intentionally. Cuts heal. Broken bones heal. Bruises heal. Psyches heal. Pain lessens. Victims forget. Move on. Get over it.

Ask yourself later, if you had to reach Piotr Malek, would you do what I did to get to him?

The weak seek out weakness. The wounded attack the wounds in others.

Surveillance is difficult on his house in Maidenhead. The neighboring land is owned by some kind of Turkish ambassador as a summer retreat so there are cameras set up along the length of it in a multi-acre hedge on both sides of the road. I rent a black BMW SUV and drive along the road twice, going and coming after stopping at a Sainsbury's, so it looks like my reconnaissance has a purpose.

Malek has a black iron gate blocking entry to his mansion, and one of his guards stands at the seam of it, unsmiling, at attention, eyeing me both times I pass.

I give him a two finger wave as I go by the second time.

I want him to remember me.

—⚏—

Inside the window of a sandwich shop, I sit at the counter, just left of the door, when Madeleine spots me. She catches herself, unsure it's me, and then waves and steps inside. There are many ways a contract killer can make himself invisible. There are also ways to position your body, your face, your clothing, put them all in motion in just the right way, to catch someone's eye.

From the doorway, she says, "I know you!"

I pretend to turn off my music and then take earbuds out of my ears.

I smile, "It's the Polish teacher."

"Yes, that's right."

The best sales jobs are when the buyer thinks she discovered the item on her own, without learning the item was placed precisely where the shop owner knew she'd look.

"Have you eaten?"

A smile pulls up the corners of her mouth and softens her face. "I haven't."

"Well, I can do better than here," I say. "What're you in the mood for?"

We walk to a sushi restaurant and take two seats at the counter.

"I should've asked if you like sushi," she says.

"I'll eat anything."

We order rolls and nigiri from an obsequious chef and when he moves off, I turn to her. "I have to ask if you're single."

She chokes on the water she just put to her lips.

"I'm sorry," I add quickly. "I know that's terribly forward."

"No, I . . . well . . . it's interesting. Without going into detail, it's complicated. How's that?"

"Ahh, okay. I would never intrude except, well, truth be told, I couldn't stop thinking about you since yesterday, and then seeing you today was like out of one of those Richard Curtis movies, and anyway, I got swept away."

She touches my forearm. "No, Jack, listen. I *am* single but there's . . ."

"Someone else."

She nods, blushing. "Someone married. It's a cliché, I know. I don't even like him that much. It's all ghastly if you think about it. Which is why I don't."

Her accent makes the old song sound cute, at least. I can see how a middle-aged Polish man would fall for her, and I understand why she would carry on the affair, but I want to hear her say it.

"And how does *that* work?" I ask. "You have to forgive me for being nosy. I have fours sisters, so it was a gossip frenzy in my house growing up."

"You *are* forward . . ." she says, but doesn't seem to mind. It's more of an observation than an accusation. "Well, what happens is he sees me on the side without his wife knowing."

"And what do you get out of it?"

"I get to live in London in a pretty nice flat that an English tutor could ill afford. It's not as romantic as a Richard Curtis film, but it's the way it is. For me, at least. An affair of convenience."

"He may not feel as flippant about it as you."

The sushi chef leans over with two plates of nigiri, a thimble of wasabi, and a bird's nest of ginger. "Salmon. Tuna. Yellowtail," he says with a British accent.

Madeleine pulls wooden chopsticks from a paper sleeve and goes to work. "So," she says between bites. "Does my scarlet letter turn you away? Because I understand if it does."

"I'm a little shocked is all."

"There's a Polish expression. *Modli się pod figurą, a diabła ma za skórą.* Roughly it translates to 'She prays but has a devil under the skin.' I always liked that one."

The sushi chef clears out our empty trays and replaces them with fresh ones. He then puts a perfectly carved rainbow roll between us.

Madeleine's eyes light up and she does a little clap and bow. "Anyway, enough about me. What about you? You have a secret you wish to relieve yourself of?"

I shake my head. "I grew up in Boston but live here now. I've never been married but did just get out of a bad relationship. My fault. She wanted commitment and I . . . didn't."

Madeleine eyes me, a hint of crow's feet crinkling the edges of her eyes. "Wow, we're covering a lot of ground on our first date."

"Impromptu first date," I say, as Madeleine polishes off the rest of the roll. I think I had one piece.

"Now," she purrs, "do you want another roll or do you want to take me home and fuck me?"

I pretend to be shocked.

I make it as far as the front gate to her flat and then tell her I'm not ready, which is the truth, although she doesn't need to know the reason why.

She doesn't act hurt, doesn't plead either, just nonchalantly moves inside her door and says, "Call me when you are, Jack." She winks at me over her shoulder and disappears inside.

I will.

Just a few pieces to move around the board and then I will ring her bell.

—⁓—

Piotr Malek's sister and her wife have theater tickets and no protection. I find this so often with marks, men with price tags on their heads. They spend enormous sums on twenty-four-hour protection, go through any number of inconveniences to keep themselves safe, and then completely neglect their immediate family. I've gotten to men through their mothers and fathers, through their brothers and sisters, the occasional aunt or uncle or cousin. It's amazing how often you can get a target to drop everything and come to you simply by texting a photo of a roughed-up sibling or parent.

Gosia Malek lives in a house Piotr paid for, lives there with her wife, her two short-hair cats, and illusions of security: dead-bolt locks, door alarms, window stoppers. The house has motion detectors but they don't turn them on because of the cats. The alarm companies love to say the motion detectors are gauged to ignore pets, but a couple of false alarms and the owners stop setting them.

I know Gosia and her wife are at the theater because the two women shouted the address at the cab driver as he pulled to the curb to pick them up. Twenty minutes later and I'm looking at a picture of the two of them posted to Instagram, smiling in front of the theater sign at the Old Vic. There has simply never been an easier time for thieves and killers. Bless you vanity. Bless you social media.

I have plenty of time to pick the lock, dismantle the alarm, and have my run of the place. On the second floor, I find Gosia's laptop. There's no code to access the desktop, so I browse through her email account. There are only five or six messages between Piotr and her, and they're written in Polish. I use Google's translator to unlock the words and though I can't trust the translation to capture nuance, it seems the emails are basic requests for money with no "How are yous" or "Tell me about your days" or "I love yous."

It seems brother and sister have a civil relationship and nothing more.

I search through drawers and cabinets, but the house is sterile, like a museum. If the cats are here, they're hiding. There's barely a sign two women live in this house, very few personal items. It's as though Gosia is more of a caretaker than an owner. Her presence in the house is as an employee for her brother, someone to watch the place while he lives in the country.

She's not a strong route to get to her brother, but that doesn't mean she can't be useful.

—⁓—

The weak target the weak. The wounded attack the wounds of others.

Olmstead meets me in a furnished flat in King's Cross and hands me the keys. The place is spare, on the first floor, down from the sidewalk, with no security except for a lock on the door. "Acceptable?" he asks.

"Perfect."

I hand him a Post-it note with a crude drawing on it. He appraises my rough sketch, and I see he's intrigued. "How soon you thinking then?"

"Tomorrow."

"Afternoon's fine?"

"Earlier the better."

"One o'clock then. You'll be here?"

"Yep."

He tugs the front of his tweed cap and jogs up the steps to Field Street before he disappears into the pedestrian crowd. I peer around at the simple furniture, the thick walls, the lack of personal detail.

When they come, I'll only need to sell them for a second.

When they come, I'll be ready, though not the way they're thinking.

—⁘—

The spring is an important part of a trap, the bait is too, but they're both worthless if the trap is not properly camouflaged.

The weak target the weak. The wounded attack the wounds in others.

Gosia parks a Land Rover and approaches her house in Clifton Villas from the north, on the path that borders the canal. I lurch from between a pair of parked cars and block her way. She stutter-steps and looks up from the glow of her phone to see what foul creature stepped into her path.

"He's a shithead," I bark at her, and Gosia has me pegged as a crazy person. She gives me a wide berth as she returns to her phone, but I block her path again and she reels from the alcohol on my breath. "He's fucking her and he's a shithead and I'll, I'll, I'm gonna do something about it!"

She stops and pulls her purse strap tight to her shoulder.

"Step away," she commands in a Polish-accented hiss, and I slyly smile, trying to play it as creepy as I can.

"I know him. I know *you*."

She's had enough. She holds her hands in front of her as though she's stumbling around in the dark, warding off evil, ready for anything, and she hisses again, "I mean it. I'll call the police."

"I know you, *Gosia*."

She stops cold. "What'd you say?"

"Gosia. Sister of Piotr. Piotr, who is fucking my girlfriend Madeleine!"

She studies me, looking for some recognition, but she's stumped.

"You tell him . . ." I let out a belch and theatrically wipe the back of my arm across my shiny lips. "You tell him if I see him, he's a dead man. You tell your brother *that*!"

"You need to go, mister."

"Mister Walker," I say to her loudly, drawing stares from windows now. "Better yet, you tell him Jack Walker on Field Street in King's Cross. Tell him to come so I can kick him in the ass."

I drunkenly kick the air.

She flinches.

With a speed she can't see coming, I grab her throat, my hands digging red blooms into her neck, and I get an inch from her face so my hot, stinking breath will be remembered for a long time. "You tell him I'll kill him."

She reacts as I hope and shoves me away, hard. I stumble back and smash my hand into a parked car with a loud thump, so loud I might've put a dent into the rear door, and then I wince, howling, cradling my left arm in my right.

"AAAHHH!" I scream, saliva flying.

She spits back at me, her face twisted with rage, "Stay away from me!" but she's not waiting around to see if I'll recover. She hurries by, casting cautious glances over her shoulder as she rounds the corner to her street.

A couple of neighbors cross the road toward me, but I growl at them and hustle away, holding my limp arm across my chest as I flee.

—៣—

Madeleine's eyes widen when she sees me in her doorway. "Aww, what happened?"

"Fractured my arm being an idiot."

"Oh, you poor baby," she says, and ushers me into her flat.

My forearm is in a plaster cast, just the fingers and thumb protruding from the gap above my palm.

"Come inside, come inside. Let me take care of you."

I move into the tiny living room, decorated as if a teenage girl lives here, all bright colors and soft lighting and poster art on the walls.

"I'm fine, thanks for inviting me over. I wasn't sure if you would answer my text."

"No, no, of course I wanted to see you. I've been—"

A second woman steps into the room, putting my plan in jeopardy or at least making it a little messier.

"This is my roommate, Sarah."

Sarah smiles at me, a Cheshire cat's smile, a canary-swallowing smile. She has dark eye shadow and dark lashes and dyed black hair and a tiny head above a too-long neck so she looks like a raccoon hiding in a hollowed-out tree trunk. "This is the one," she says, and it sounds sexual the way she says it, practiced, like she could take any four words and make them lewd.

"Nice to meet you," I say, but my thoughts are recalculating like a GPS system when you take a wrong turn and the map needs a few seconds to find a new route.

"I'm not staying," Sarah says, as if she reads my thoughts. "So you can relax and get what you came for."

"Oh, stop," Madeleine squeaks.

"Call me if you need anything. I'll just be at the Hopper."

"Will do, love."

Sarah gives me one last seductive look and is out the door. Her footsteps recede.

Recalculating. Recalculating.

The weak target the weak. The wounded attack the wounds of others.

"Something to drink?"

"Sure."

I need to wait a few minutes, fifteen to be safe, make sure Sarah doesn't come back for a forgotten scarf or a hat or keys.

"Whiskey?"

"Sure."

She clinks a couple of ice cubes into a highball glass and pours from a bottle of Jameson. Not my brand but I'll work with what I have. I take the glass and sip.

She pours herself the same drink and downs it like a shot, refills it.

"Sarah's fine. She's staying here for what was supposed to be two weeks and is going on a year. We take care of each other. She was attending nursing school but that might be put on hold. She works at a jewelry store, not nice jewelry but a little better than costume, yeah?" She holds up a hand to her ear. "Like these."

I look at a pair of strange loops that vaguely resemble Saturn.

"Do you want to sit on the couch?"

I look at my watch and it's time. I take no pleasure in what I'm about to do, but the doctor takes no pleasure in plunging a needle through the skin, no pleasure in snapping a bone into place. It's a painful means to a painful end but the weak target the weak and the wounded attack the wounds of others.

"I don't like you with that man," I say, and take a step forward.

She stops cold, blinks. "What?"

"The man. The Polish man."

"What the fuck're you on ab——" but before she finishes the sentence, I devastate her with a right cross that rises out of nowhere like a summer storm whipping across a farm. She reels back, equal parts shocked and in pain, like she innocently reached into a sleeping bag and a scorpion stung her.

"What are you——" but I hit her again, this time with my left, my cast, and she flips onto her back as though I pulled a rug out from underneath her feet.

I jerk back, holding my cast across my chest with my right hand, in pain. A scream gurgles in her throat, wells up for a foghorn blast, her face distorted with anger and fear and confusion, inflamed, and then she lets it go, a wail, a head-splitting, eardrum-shaking shriek with a higher pitch and more force than I thought could escape a human throat.

I don't need to do any more damage, this is enough, her purple eye, her cut cheek, her split lip are enough. She raises her feet and kicks wildly in my direction, slashing the air and flailing without pause. Her scream only grows in strength, and I hurry out the door, pulling my hoodie over my head because though I do want to get caught, I want to pay for this, not here and not by a good Samaritan.

I want Malek's men to come for me.

—⚏—

The air is still in the flat below Field Street.

I can see what is happening as easily as if it were playing on a stage in front of me. Madeleine's roommate, Sarah, comes home and finds her friend disheveled on the floor, her cuts bleeding, her eye swelling, and there are some "Oh my Gods" and "That bastards" and Madeleine climbs to her feet, infuriated.

Sarah pulls up her cell to dial 999 but Madeleine stops her, grabs the phone out of her hand, and says "No, no, no," and Sarah pleads "Maddy, honey, we have to call the police," and Madeleine repeats "*No!*" pounding the word like a flat black key on a piano, and Sarah says "But that prick can't get away with this," and Madeleine turns her red-hot eyes on her roommate and growls "He won't."

And then she calls Piotr.

—⁓—

I'm in the bathroom when they come.

I wasn't planning to be. I was going to stand in the kitchen, my back to the door, stirring a pot of spaghetti, caught off guard, that was my plan.

But I had to take a piss. So I took a break to relieve myself, finished, and I'm washing my good hand in the sink when the front door is kicked off its hinges.

I'm caught flat-footed, vulnerable, but I still put up a fight.

I was going to scald one of them with the spaghetti water so they'd be extra pissed later but lucky for them, I'm away from the stove.

I make a good show of fighting back, get a few elbows and knuckles into the taller of the two, maybe break his nose, but I didn't hear it crack so I'm not sure.

Finally, the other one gets my good arm behind my back while the taller one throws a couple of right crosses to my head. The problem with playing possum is that I keep getting my jaw realigned, my face pummeled. It's a strategy that has its drawbacks; namely, it's fucking painful, and my ability to handle it has receded over time. I hang my head, go limp. It doesn't take much of an act.

They slap me awake, march me through the apartment, up the short flight of stone steps, banging my forehead into the metal railing for good measure, then force me into the back of a town car, where a third thug is waiting with a gun cocked.

He puts it to my temple, and if I miscalculated, then this is the end of it, the end of me, but the weak target the weak and the wounded attack the wounds in others.

—◦—

I sit in a chair in a linoleum-tiled room, a drain in the floor beneath my feet, blood dripping into its metal maw from a wound where my teeth cut into my lip. Rain jackets, thick coats, hats, scarves, and gloves hang from hooks on the walls; galoshes and hiking boots scatter the floor. A weed eater, garden shears, gloves, and a looping green garden hose rest on shelves in the corner.

The space is wide, kitchen-size, and light filters in from the glass inside a door in the corner. This is a "mudroom," a place to kick off all your rainy, dirt-caked, soiled gear after you come in from the garden or the back fields or the dirt trails outside the house in Maidenhead.

There's a large sink and a small coil of hose next to it, along with a steel brush, for getting the bigger chunks of mud from old boots. Three men crowd the room, surrounding me like a wolf pack, the two who worked me over when they seized me, and the third who held the gun to my head. He's still fisting his weapon.

They're waiting for the boss. No one bothers to hand me a cloth to let me put pressure to the cuts on my face. They want to show the boss what they've done, that they've followed orders. They're puppies yearning for pats on the head. Good boys, good.

I look them over but don't say a word. They didn't cuff my hands. They don't have my feet tied to the chair. They think I'm the idiot who manhandled the boss's mistress. They think they have strength in numbers. They're half of the six-man unit from Polish Special Forces here to protect Piotr Malek, but he or they are making the mistake made by so many confident men: using defensive weapons for offense.

My arms hang limply from my shoulder, the left forearm hanging low from the weight of the cast.

The air stirs as the other three guards enter, followed by the man himself, Piotr Malek in the flesh, finally, his face a topography map of wrinkles, his eyes dark and intense, like black holes to his soul, sucking light and life from the room. He's the alpha wolf, the predator, the carnivore, but at his core he's a weak, spiteful man who marches defenseless men into an oven and burns them alive.

The mudroom is large but this many bodies strains its capacity and the air thickens and warms, like inside a greenhouse. The men form a circle around me, schoolyard bullies waiting to get a few kicks in on the defenseless weakling.

The weak target the weak. The wounded attack the wounds of others.

Piotr Malek kneels in front of me and wipes his fingers in the blood collected in the grate at the top of the drain. He examines the red tips of his fingers then rubs them into his thumb like he's rubbing away grease or dried glue. His eyes find mine and try to consume them.

"Do you know who I am?" he asks, always the prelude to a beating.

"You're the dickless prick who is fucking my girl," I respond.

Instead of enraged, he seems amused. "You harass my sister, then you give a black eye to a girl you just met, and I can't help but think this is your plan, yes? To meet me? And you think I would fall for this ruse, for this absurd bullshit, yes?"

I don't say anything, but the wheels turn in my head. Recalculating, recalculating.

"Is he armed?" he asks the man nearest him in Polish, the one who has the gun to my head, and that one answers, "No," or at least I think that's the exchange they make, but my Polish isn't too good. I could use a tutor.

"So here I am, you've met me," he spreads his arms wide and two of his men take a step back to give him room, like actors yielding the stage to a soliloquist. "Now what, you piece of garbage? You want to come at me? You want to smash that broken wing into my face? Is that what you want? I'm right here."

The tension in the room boils as though someone cranks the dial on a stovetop. All of Malek's men are poised, none more so than the one with the gun cocked in my face. I think each of them wants me to try, wants me to lunge for their boss, because the weak target the weak and the wounded attack the wounds in others.

The way I die is *not* in a mudroom bought and paid for with the burning flesh of political dissidents.

"No?" Malek asks as he struts like a red-tipped rooster. "No? Nothing to say? Then I'll ask you two questions. Who are you and who do you work for?"

I glare at him balefully, like I'm having a hard time keeping my eyelids open. When he thinks I'm not going to answer, I whisper softly.

"What'd you say? What'd he say?" he asks, but his men shake their heads. No one could hear me.

I raise my chin up, meet his eyes. "I said, *Strzep sobie kapucyna*," which roughly translates to "Go jerk yourself." I'm not sure if I got the pronunciation correct, but it's close enough to make Malek's eyes shimmer like a heat cloud passes between us. Then he wallops me with enough force to tip my chair over so I fall on the floor like a ship capsizing after a rogue wave.

I land hard on my side and his eyes light on my cast and his boot comes down hard on it, a weak man targeting my weakness, a wounded man attacking my wound, and I scream to make it seem right, and I reach my right hand over to knock his boot away, a natural reaction for someone who has his broken arm crunched under a boot, but my arm is not broken, it was never injured, I never cracked it on the side of a car in front of his sister. No, instead, in the disarray of Malek stomping my forearm and in the confusion of my screaming and flailing and what can only be taken for a pathetic attempt to protect my wounded limb, I jam my right-hand fingers into the opening Olmstead designed when he built this cast and the plaster breaks up along two fault lines built into the hard white structure so the cover falls off completely. In that instant, I have my Glock in my hand and the element of surprise on my side.

I shoot the one holding the gun before he realizes what happened so his face has no reaction when it caves in on itself. Blood and brain spatter into the eyes of the two men flanking him, the ones who pummeled me in the flat on Field Street, so I drop them with the next two shots before they have time to wipe their eyes.

I've learned in these situations—when bullets fly in close quarters—it's best to keep in perpetual motion. If you stop or freeze or pause, bullets find you.

I dive toward the three fallen bodyguards, away from the three others, and Piotr Malek still has half a plaster cast under his boot and stares down at it like he's trying to understand how the magician went from the cabinet to the stage wing.

I wedge my body between two of the capsized bodies, using them like sandbags in a World War II bunker, and site on Malek but one of his men actually steps in front of him and takes the bullet. I have no idea who this man is or what psychological shortcoming compelled him to sacrifice his life for his boss's like he's in the goddamned secret service, but this is the first time in my long career I've seen a hired man act as a human shield for the scumbag who pays him a weekly wage. Good for you, moron. I'm honestly impressed. Mystified, but impressed.

The remaining gunmen pull Berettas from shoulder holsters and spray ammunition while they back toward the outside door, screaming in Polish. What they're saying I have no idea. Malek turns his back on me and bolts like a rabbit trying to escape a coyote. He doesn't wait to see if his guards cover him or lead him out, he just grabs a pair of garden shears off a hook as he runs out the door.

I scissor my legs with my torso to the floor, gun arm extended at the guards so my body moves in an arc, and I fire three more times. Two bullets catch the two guards, one in the chest, the other in the neck, and they flop to the linoleum, jerking like fish reeled into a boat. My third bullet embeds in the door next to Malek's head, but he's through it, unscathed, dashing to freedom. Shit.

Six guards dropped in a mudroom on a rich man's estate because the weak target the weak and the wounded attack the wounds in others. At least there's a drain built into the floor for whoever has to come clean this mess.

I leap to my feet and follow Malek out the door without breaking stride, and if he were experienced in gun fighting, he would have waited for me to move from inside to outside, waited for the moment when my eyes have to adjust to the light, waited to ambush me and put a bullet in my head. But Malek is a man who leads handcuffed prisoners into ovens, not a man who knows how to waylay his enemy in a firefight.

I glimpse him as he dashes through the door of what must be the garage, and I sprint for it. The game will change completely if he escapes his property, if he can go to ground like a rodent burrowing in a hole, shore up his defenses, reload, rearm, recalculate.

I kick open the door and ten panes of glass in its center shatter when it claps back against the wall. My irises have to dilate again because it is dark inside. There are four vehicles parked here, two sports cars plus a big SUV and an even bigger Suburban, eenie, meenie, minie, moe, but the garage door is closed.

I spy a stairwell leading to my left and realize this is a two-story garage. If I were Malek, I would've gone for the Suburban, but maybe the keys are upstairs?

Jostling above me, like furniture sliding across the floor; I don't wait for more, I know what he's doing, trying to barricade himself in until help arrives, so I bound up the stairs and hit the door at the top with my full impact, like a football blocker picking up a linebacker crossing over the middle, and I arrive in the nick of time.

He is sliding a large dresser across the door but hasn't gotten it in place. When I hit the door, the dresser pushes back on a pivot and I'm in the room, angry now, thirsty, letting all of it rise, front and center, the prisoners incinerated to death, the kidnapping of Matthew Boone's son, all out and in front of me where I can see it.

His lips tighten and pull back, revealing rows of tiny teeth, sharp little shards like gravel on a hot rooftop. His eyes are feral, the exertion of dashing to this room and trying to move the dresser too much for a murderous, snarling old man.

The room is a caretaker's quarters—a studio flat, kitchen, living room, bedroom, work bench all in one—a big open space above the master's garage and here is the master in a room he probably hasn't set foot in since it was built. He snatches up the gardening shears and holds the blades out in front of him like a knight's apprentice trying to raise a sword too big for him.

I show him my gun and he lowers the shears but keeps both hands on the handles so his arms dangle in front of him. "I have money. I . . ." he says, but stops, ashamed. This is the entreaty of cowards, and he realizes it as soon as the words are out of his mouth. "You. Who are you?"

"The killer you should've hired."

He hangs his head, then looks back up at me.

"I'm not going to grovel but I can pay you now if that's what this is about. Pay you more than I paid him."

He drops the garden shears so they clatter on the floor. "No, no, I can see this is not about money for you so . . ."

He waves a hand feebly in the air. His eyes search for a place to sit, but the sofa is too far away so even this dignity eludes him. "I'm old. I've lived my life. Get on with it."

"I refuse," I say, and he looks at me, puzzled. I lower my gun because I like him off-balance. It's an executioner's play . . . give the condemned man a glimpse of freedom and he might give up his secrets before he's marched to the noose.

Malek looks past me to the door, back down at the garden shears, calculating probabilities, the old engineer's mind revving to find a solution to a shifting problem. He was resigned to die, but now, a ray of sunlight.

"If you don't mean to kill me, then what's all this about?"

"You tell me."

He exaggerates a shoulder shrug, which would make me chuckle under different circumstances. As it stands, it fuels my disgust.

"I mean I don't know," and his Polish accent kicks in thicker, like the words come from deep in his sternum. "I mean you say that I should have hired you, but I don't know what this means. You couldn't—"

"Matthew Boone."

His eyes try to read my expression as a fresh wave of defeat washes over him.

"Fine. Fine. I wanted him dead and he hired you to do the same to me, fine. I lost, he won . . . yes, I should've hired you."

Something is not right here, something that begins to ring like an alarm bell in my head.

"Be done with it," the old man continues. "If you're going to shoot me, shoot me. Just be done with it." He paces in two-step bursts, like a kite on the end of a string, twisting in the wind.

"That's it?" I say and lower the gun again, and I can tell it's starting to get to him, the twists between certain death and glimmers of hope.

"What do you want?" he gasps, to me or to God, I'm not sure, and then his legs give and he sits down heavily on the floor next to the garden shears, giving them no more than a feverish glance. Yes, something is definitely wrong.

"You know I don't want your money."

"Yes, I see that."

"Then don't you have something you want to negotiate with?"

He searches my face for meaning, trying to solve the riddle but the answer is hidden.

"I have money, I have cars, I have *things*." Then his mind seizes on an idea. "I have influence. I have friends in Poland, in Russia, yes? You have someone there who needs help. Yes, I can help your friend if he—"

"I don't have friends."

His mouth snaps shut and his lips tighten again. "You're cruel," he groans, studying his hands, turning them inside and out like kids used to do. "You're cruel. You want something but you won't say what it is. You're going to kill me, you won't do it. You say Matthew Boone hired you, but it doesn't matter, a hundred people want me dead, and I outlived most of them so psssh, it's all borrowed time."

"You have something I want," I say, but I'm beginning to think he doesn't.

"Then name it, you bastard. You miserable son of a bitch, name it!" and spittle sprays from his mouth, no pretense of remaining calm, cool, collected.

"Why did you want to kill Matthew Boone?"

"He wouldn't sell me his software."

"And killing him would—"

"There are others in his company who are amenable."

"What do you need with facial recognition?"

"I'm just a broker."

"Russia?"

Malek nods. "Russia cannot match the technological advancements of the West. They never have. Have you seen a Russian power plant? Imagine that lack of innovation and apply it to all sectors of government. One thing Russia has always been good at is stealing. You don't have to be technologically advanced if you steal the advances from others. So if I could facilitate such a theft, why should I not make profit?"

I shake my head because nothing he's saying adds up to why I'm here in the first place, why I didn't just shoot Malek when I smashed through this door, and the fact that he can't see it, that he didn't even bring it up, means I'm the one who played this wrong.

"Was it Ezra Loeb who arranged this? He collects money from me and from Matthew Boone, puts the two bets against each other and takes his cut whether he dies or I—"

"Where's Josh?"

"Who?"

"Matthew Boone's son? Josh?"

"What do you mean?"

"You don't know."

It's not a question. I understand now.

He sees it at the same time. "Ahh, I understand. Matthew Boone's son has been kidnapped and your charge is to get the boy back. It makes sense now, yes. Okay. Okay. I can help you if you'll—"

But I shoot him at close range, one shot through the middle of his head. He topples over like a yard sign caught in a gust of wind.

He didn't know, which means he didn't order it, which means whoever took Josh did not get his strings pulled by Piotr Malek.

This London trip is, literally and figuratively, a dead end.

10

The return flight is into the wind and thus longer, and since I need to stave off jet lag, I stay up for the duration, thinking.

There are no coincidences in this business, none I've ever seen. Sure, you might get lucky and walk up on a mark as he's changing a flat tire or you might expect an army of bodyguards and find your target alone, oblivious, taking a morning shower, completely vulnerable, but that's not coincidence. Fortunate, yes, a gift from the heavens, oh yeah, but not a perfect concomitance of unrelated events.

Therefore, Josh's kidnapping and the hit on his father are related. The man who ordered the hit did not order the kidnapping. That is true. I saw it with my own eyes and need no outside confirmation. So who else is involved? The hit man Keith Watts, but he was drawing his last breath in a state park parking lot when Josh was taken. Ezra Loeb, but he insists he didn't hire more than one shooter, and though he's a practiced liar, I believe him. He had no reason to lie about it, didn't mention it when he had the chance. Besides, Malek would've known about it and definitely didn't.

And if the kidnappers were using the abduction to draw out Matthew Boone, why no demands and why not kill Boone when they had him dead to rights?

My head starts to throb and I remember to drink some water. The weak target the weak. The answer is here somewhere, but the pain in my head darkens and I close my eyes for a few seconds to decrease the stimuli, to ease the tension, and the next time I open them is as the captain dings the bell to let us know arrival is imminent.

—◆—

The house on Cedar Creek Road is as somber as a cemetery and it's time to move. I was gone six days and still zero contact from the men holding Josh so there's no reason to stay. Archie talked to Ezra Loeb and he swears on his life the kidnapping order didn't come from any fence, hitter, or client in the known underworld. It's a rogue job. His lack of answers squares with what I know.

Archie, Matthew Boone, and Peyton searched the farmhouse top to bottom, inspected the surrounding woods too, making sure the kidnappers didn't dump Josh at the scene. They came up empty, a blessing.

Matthew Boone seems to have aged another decade since I left, lines around his mouth and eyes are wider, deeper, as though rivers have flowed through and eroded the bedrock.

We use the dining room like a conference table, no fire in the fireplace. The room holds no warmth. Boone has his head lowered and keeps rubbing his hands over his pate like he's trying to contain bad thoughts from escaping.

"I keep listening and I keep listening to you and it gets us nothing," he says in a perfectly reasonable voice, but I know what volcanic earthquakes sound like before an eruption.

I keep my own volume level. "Who at your office would make decisions in your absence?"

He looks up at me like the question came from another planet.

"What?"

"Who in your office is most likely to make decisions if you're not there to make them?"

"My CFO Donald Blake. I told you I trust him. What's this have to—"

"He sold you out."

"What?"

"He sold you out," I repeat.

Boone shakes his head, a child not getting the answer he wants when he asks for a later bedtime or more ice cream. "Donald's a good man. I've known him fifteen years."

"He made a deal with Piotr Malek. If you're gone from the company, he'll sell him the software. The Russians want it, Malek was their broker, only you wouldn't play ball. They made a deal with your second-in-command."

"But he can't—"

"Can't what?"

"Can't sell it without me."

"He did."

"No, you don't understand. I'm the only one who knows the encryption key to unlock it. He can't just sell it. It's useless without the . . ." He stops, everything falling into place. "That's why they took Josh. That's what they want to exchange. The encryption codes to unlock the software for my son."

"Does Donald have a military history?"

"I don't think so. He's an MBA from somewhere in the South."

"University of Texas," Peyton inserts. "He wears a Longhorns golf shirt to work every now and then."

"He look military to you?"

Peyton shrugs, scrunches up her nose. "I don't think so."

"Why?" Boone asks, but I'm turning to Archie.

"Can you get us everything you can on Donald Blake while we switch safe houses?"

Archie nods. "On it," and he's out the door.

"Why?" Boone asks again. "Why do you keep asking if he's military?"

"I want to know if he hired someone directly to kidnap your son or if he did it himself."

"No way it was him—" then he stops suddenly, looking over my shoulder, and I turn to see Liam in the doorway, face ashen. Boone stands and gathers himself, though he looks as though he could blow apart at any moment. "Liam. Go to bed, son."

But Liam steps into the room, his chin out, defiant. "Why haven't you found Josh?"

He looks at the three adults, accusing. "He's just a little kid. Why haven't you . . ." and his voice catches in his throat and he lets out a heartbreaking, "God!" His lip quivers but he keeps his eyes dry.

"Liam," his dad repeats, tired.

Liam jerks his eyes to his father.

"What? What?! More nothing! More nothing! It's a *joke!*" and he spins and dashes from the room, pounds up the stairs and from somewhere above, a door slams.

Boone peers down at the table, his head a heavy weight. Peyton eyes me, then flicks her gaze up the stairs, silently asking me if she should go give the boy comfort. I don't respond so she rolls her eyes, sick of me, sick of all of it, and I hear her feet following Liam's up the stairs.

I'm not going to comfort that kid. I'm not going to say a word to him. I'm not going to let this father off the hook. It's his problem, not mine. If I can reunite him with his son, so be it, but if caring is part of the bargain, then cut me out now because caring died for me under a covered bridge in Massachusetts. Caring died for me at a roadside diner outside Chicago. I see clearly what Archie tried to do, see it as clearly as if he had written it in fifty-foot letters, see it for what it is: a misguided attempt to make me care about this family since I could not care for my own.

I will not. I cannot.

I am a killer not a protector, a sword not the armor, a goddamn gun not a bulletproof vest.

I am Columbus.

I am not Copeland.

I cannot wear that suit. It doesn't fit.

—⁓—

I stand outside the room, silent in the hallway, eavesdropping for no reason I can reconcile. Peyton soothes, like a new mother calming an infant in the crib.

"I'll tell you something I read in a book once. You ever seen something that was so right you just wanted to take a picture of it and hold on to it. A flower? A bird? A pretty girl? Well, this quote was like that . . . it was so real, I knew I had to memorize it. You ready? It went like this: 'Life is neither good nor evil, but only a *place* for good and evil.' A guy named Marcus Aurelius wrote that a long time ago, and what he meant was you're born into a world that isn't black, isn't white, it's gray. Your parents can try to keep the evil out, they can try to protect you from it, keep the doors locked, keep the lights on, but this world is a place for good and evil. Sometime it's inside the room with us, *in* us, and sometimes, it's out there, waiting for us, and we have to deal with it when it comes. That's what we're doing now, we're dealing with the evil of the world—me, your dad, Mr. Copeland, Archie, we're dealing with it and you have to also. You didn't do anything to bring about this evil. It just is. Life is a place for good and evil. You see?"

"You fight it with good?"

"Sometimes. Most of the time. You see someone doing evil, you fight it with good. That's the answer I should tell you. That's where I should stop. But you're old enough to hear the truth, Liam. And the truth is, sometimes you fight evil with evil."

"Is that what you're doing?"

"Yes."

"My dad too?"

"I can't speak for him."

"But you'll do it?"

"Yes."

"I want to help."

"I know you do. And I won't tell you that you can't. That's for you to decide. And listen, since I'm speaking the truth, that's *not* for your dad to decide, no matter what he tells you, that's for *you* to decide. But I'll be honest, the chances that you would hurt *our* chances of defeating this evil are high. You may mean to help, but you could end up hurting. And I don't want that, but again, that's for you to decide. The best thing you can do is to stay here, stay safe, and let us do the evil for you. Do you understand?"

Liam nods and says something, but I can't make out the words.

I thought Peyton was a natural, but I didn't know she was this wise. What I was taught about the nature of what I do she picked up innately. Hell, she can explain it better to an eleven-year-old than I explained it to her.

She has a career ahead of her when this is over, if she's alive.

Matthew Boone ascends the stairs behind me. I have no guilt on my face for eavesdropping because I don't feel guilty. I was meant to hear that.

He passes me, unconcerned, and moves into the room, holding a plate of sandwiches.

After a moment, Peyton emerges. She stops short when she sees me, then meets my eyes, taking ownership of the words she knows I overheard.

—⁂—

We travel to a cabin across the state line into Washington. The trip is short, and we ride in silence. I drive, Peyton rides shotgun, and Boone sits in the back with Liam. The sky is its usual gray, a flat, endless ceiling. The landscape along the highway is green and lush, the forest dense. Every direction seems to push in on you, a compactor closing around garbage.

The puzzle pieces are locking into place, but one piece doesn't fit. Malek wanted Boone dead so he could deal with Donald Blake. Blake doesn't have the encryption codes to unlock the software, so it wouldn't make sense to kill Boone before he had them, hence the kidnapping.

Either Malek or Blake didn't have all the information.

Archie meets us at the end of a dirt drive in a newly rented Range Rover. He unlocks a chain stretched across the throat of a side path, then secures the padlock after we drive onto the dirt road. Signs along the road on our way here warned us the path was closed and patrolled by armed security, ostensibly to keep out hikers and backpackers. We have the land to ourselves.

The cabin is a smaller, shabbier, no-frills affair tucked against the side of a hill back from the road. It only has two bedrooms with two sets of bunk beds in each so it sleeps eight. Peyton wrinkles her nose and chooses the left room.

"Y'all can sleep in there," she says, and tosses her sack onto a bed. "This one's mine."

Archie looks at me and shrugs his shoulders.

"What'd you find?" I ask.

"A lot," he says, and opens a file, spreading out pages on a long wooden table with scratches all over its surface.

—⁂—

Donald Blake's résumé prior to working for Popinjay reads like a monument to the new millennium. Following his time at the University of Texas, he worked in the oil and gas business, with stints in IT and accounting at Shell and Exxon. He lived in Austin and Midland and Odessa and Houston and traveled to Saudi Arabia, Kuwait, the United Arab Emirates, and Qatar. Staid, traditional work wasn't his ambition though, so in 1999, he leapt to the nascent Internet industry and landed an early executive post at Amazon, where he should've stayed. Instead, he made a poor decision to head up finance at Pets.com. It bankrupted him, and according to court papers, cost him his marriage as well.

On his ass for six months, contacted by a headhunter—great name for the job, by the way—he was tossed a lifeline by Matthew Boone. He's been with the company since 2002, has never remarried, and rents a residence apartment in the heart of downtown Portland, on the fourteenth floor of the Yamhill Hotel overlooking Pioneer Square, about four blocks from the Morrison Bridge. He has no wife, no kids, but a bank account that says he likes to spend. I don't have time to find out whether his money is in a bookie's pockets or up his nose.

If I had to put my finger on his personality type, I'd say he's one of those guys who feels *owed*, who feels the world gave him the short straw but he deserves more. He deserves the front page, the corner office, the mansion, the Bentley. The world has conspired to hold him back, hold him down, right?

Maybe this plot was his attempt to seize the crown.

Boone looks up from the file in disbelief. "I've sat at the conference table with Donald Blake countless times. We'd walk to the food trucks together. He helped me negotiate the first big sale Popinjay ever had. The man you're describing here is not the man I know."

"I pulled his cell records. He's—"

"How could you do that? You'd have to have a warrant."

Archie looks at Matthew Boone like he's a child.

"Tell him," he says to me.

"Archie is one of the best fences in the world. This is what he does."

"Believe that," Archie adds.

"But it's impossible if you don't have a judge who . . ."

"Motherfucker, you ever hear of a bribe? *Everyone* has a price. Everyone. And if you got a Fed you trust and a judge or two who like to buy lake houses or fly private or go on goddamn safaris, you think it's hard to get phone records? Shiiiiit. Please."

It's always funny to watch Archie get worked up. Reminds me of the old days.

"As I was saying," and he pauses to give Boone the stink eye to see if he wants to interrupt again. When he doesn't, Archie waits a little longer to make him pay for challenging him. Finally, he continues, "I got a hold of his phone records. He made fifteen calls to London last month. I don't need to tell you who he called 'cause you already know. If we'd've had more time, we would've drawn the line to him sooner."

Boone's face reddens and he focuses on a spot behind me, a thousand yards away. "Where is Donald now?"

"Apparently he's skipped work this week, since the day after the kidnapping. Again, something that would've raised a red flag if we were looking in that direction, but . . ." and Archie lets the sentence die.

We're both out of our element here. We're used to acquiring a target, researching the mark, and then putting the man into the ground. We're not accustomed to discovering targets as we go, although it feels good to home in on one now. I have yet to lay eyes on Donald Blake, but I can feel the seed of hatred start to sprout, take root, bloom. A man who couldn't find a legitimate path to success so he tried to force a different route? A Trojan horse, sitting back, smiling, waiting for another man's murder to propel him into the CEO's chair. Yes, he isn't going to be hard to hate.

The way I die is consumed by righteous fire.

"I want to talk to him," Boone says. "Let me talk to him."

Archie shakes his head. "We're past that."

"I have to see his face. He has to look me in the eye."

"Can't do it."

"Dammit! He came at *me*, Archie! He came at me! I've been sitting in a cage for weeks and I want to look him in the eye and tell him I know what he's done. And I want to ask him why. He was at Meredith's funeral for Chrissake. I took him in because I believed in him. I want to ask him *Why?* How? How he could do this to me?"

"Do you want your son back?" I interrupt.

His eyes find me. "Yes," he growls.

"I'll get him back." I feel Archie and Peyton's eyes on each side of my head, boring holes there, entry and exit wounds.

"How?" he asks hoarsely.

"I won't be asking Donald Blake why, I can promise you that."

—m—

Matthew Boone looks more at peace than I've seen him. He asks what the plan is and I tell him. He tells me it's okay to leave him alone now . . . no one can possibly know this new safe house, and he understands what we have to do. After reading the file on Blake, he's wrapped his head around the betrayal.

I leave him Archie's keys to the Range Rover in case he needs to get away in a hurry, and he takes them with steady hands.

Archie believes Donald Blake is holed up in his apartment on the fourteenth floor of the Yamhill Hotel but he isn't sure. Not one hundred percent. Blake could've run while I was across the pond, but run to where, we don't know.

Peyton knows a woman, Shelly Davis, who works at Popinjay. They occasionally eat lunch together at a sandwich shop down the street. Shelly did some sort of coding on the twenty-fourth floor and reported directly to Donald Blake, held meetings with him two or three times a week. Peyton calls her and she agrees to meet for a cup of coffee. Archie and I occupy the adjacent booth.

"The place is in total disarray. Total disarray. Everyone is walking around like a land mine is going to go off at any minute. Matthew has been gone for weeks . . . now Donald is missing. Louis Newman was murdered in the parking lot of Forest Park, did you know that?"

Peyton tells her she didn't.

"Some kind of a mugging spree. Some Portland police detectives questioned a bunch of people on twenty-five and twenty-six but left without telling anyone anything. No one knows if we're still getting paychecks. Remember Kinsey in accounting? She bailed. So did Phil. I don't even know if the company is still a company.

"Jessica Chen called a meeting to tell everyone she didn't know what the hell was happening either, but she has a cousin who works for the Seattle PD and she was going to see if he knew anyone in Portland PD she could talk to and maybe get some answers. I have kids, Peyton. I can't afford to have this job vaporize."

"I didn't know any of this. I've been out of the loop."

"Well it didn't help that everyone from security up and quit at the same time. Sure didn't make anyone feel safe. A couple of coders in the cubicles next to mine play video games all day now."

"Has Donald checked in at all?"

"I heard him on a conference call with Jessica Chen, telling her not to worry, everything would be explained soon. So they were in contact, but it's all so weird, weird, weird. What do *you* know? Why'd you quit?"

"Me? I got a job offer at a cabin chain in Washington. Sounds like I left in the nick of time. I was just thinking of you and wanted to get a bite."

They split up after that and we meet down the street at Peyton's Ford SUV.

"You catch all that?"

"Yeah. I agree with Archie. Donald Blake is holed up here, waiting to see what kind of deal he can make. It's time to knock on his door and offer him one."

—◆—

We skirt Pioneer Square and walk into the Yamhill Hotel and Residences lobby, Archie in front, Peyton behind him, and I bring up the rear. The space is warm, arty, with a white check-in counter along one wall and a sleepy bar on the other side of the lobby. A bank of elevators await travelers around the counter from the concierge desk, and a secure door in the corner has a key fob pad hanging on to the wall above a small sign that reads, "Residents Only."

Archie and I peel away from Peyton as she approaches the Registration desk and asks whom she can speak to regarding renting an apartment. We enter the elevator alcove and I push the up button. Doors spring open and I press the top floor; we keep both our chins down to avoid security cameras as the elevator elevates.

It dings open on the mezzanine, and a maid hops on, presses a middle floor, and hops off, all the while talking on her cell phone in an Eastern European language that sounds Slovenian. She never looked up from her pushcart.

On the tenth floor, the doors open again and Archie passes me, glances quickly at the fire escape route, and nods to his left. "Getting my bearings," he says, more to himself than me.

There is no one in this hallway and we hit the stairwell at the end of the hall and ascend, our footfalls echoing softly, and I feel like an engine revving, like wheels smoking, like a throttle opening. Archie, ahead of me, turns around and gives me his toothy half smile, like he senses it, too. We get to the fourteenth floor and wait.

"You ever hear the parable of the mirror?" he asks, and lights up a cigarette right here in the stairwell, cocking one eye at me as the smoke frames his head like a Renaissance savior.

"The what?"

"The parable of the mirror. It's a story that tells you—"

"I know what a goddamn parable is."

Archie takes another drag, unfazed. He points at me with the cigarette between his fingers, using it to punctuate his story. "Man buys a mirror, looks into it, doesn't like what he sees. Hair is messed up, tie isn't straight, there's lint on his shoulder, that type of thing. He reaches at the mirror, tries to fix his hair, knock the fuzz off his jacket, straighten his tie, but his fingers keep hitting the glass. He starts to yell at the reflection. 'Let me fix this! C'mon! Let me fix this!' His friend stops by and says, 'Whatchoo yelling at, brother?' The man points at the mirror, pissed. 'It won't let me fix anything,' he cries. The friend says, 'Son, you can't change the reflection, you can only change *you*.'" Archie taps his finger to his head and takes another lungful of smoke.

"The moral of the story is the guy's an idiot?"

Archie shakes his head. "Maybe. Maybe that *is* the moral."

Just then, the door to the fourteenth-floor stairwell opens and Peyton stands there, waiting for us.

"All clear," she says. "He's in 1414."

"What'd you do with the person showing you around?"

"Took his keycard and gave him the slip."

I would've liked to have seen that.

We move down the residence hallway briskly, heads down. No one steps out from a room or an elevator to note our way.

We hit the wall on either side of 1414. A security peephole looks out from the center of the door, so I knock and get ready by positioning my body directly in front of the door, one leg behind the other, balanced, low center of gravity, like a man bracing to stop a heavy boulder rolling down a hill. I would handle this differently if I were here to kill Donald Blake, but for now, I just want him to talk.

I wait, wait, engine idling. The peephole darkens and I launch a kick into the door with everything I have, aiming for the vulnerable spot right next to the handle. The door explodes, banging into Donald Blake before he has a chance to prepare himself. He caroms into a wall, rattling his head coming and going, like a pool ball ricocheting off the rails. Peepholes are great for letting intruders know exactly where you're standing.

A pack of dogs, Archie, Peyton, and I whip into the room and close the door behind us. Before Donald Blake has a chance to recover, I frog march him to a chair in the living room, away from the door. Archie turns up the TV to wash out Blake's moans, and Peyton sweeps and clears the other rooms using the training she learned when she was a cop.

Donald Blake is alone, evidence enough he's in way over his head. Rooms cleared, Peyton stands behind him while I open the door once more to see if our battering-ram entry raised any eyebrows from nosy neighbors, but the hallway is silent. Good.

Archie finds a dishrag and tosses it across the room so it smacks Blake in the face. Our victim takes his hand from where it is clamped over his left eye—the place the door caught him—and pulls back a bloody palm, then replaces it with the towel.

"The hell is this," he puffs. But he knows, it's all over his face, the way his shoulders sag. Playing dumb is the default position of anyone caught in a lie. *Huh? What? What do you mean?*

I move in front of Blake, pull him to his feet, and he hangs limply in front of me while I pat him down for a weapon. He's a businessman, though, not a killer, so I don't find anything.

I drop him back in the chair, slide over a glass coffee table, and sit down in front of him, so we're eye to eye. Archie hangs back in his blind spot, which will drive any man crazy, and Peyton slides to the door, the three of us moving in a triangle like we've done this a thousand times.

"I need your eyes on me, Donald."

Miserable, Donald Blake keeps his eyes cast down, that dishtowel held to his head by a shaky hand. I slap him in the wounded spot hard enough to rattle his teeth.

He reels back and makes a howling noise that sounds oddly like a cow's *moo*.

"You're gonna do what I say, Donald. The sooner you do, the less severe I'm gonna be."

This gets him to raise his eyes. Hatred has replaced pain.

"Good. That's step one. Where's Josh?"

"You're the one who took the place of Max Finnerich, right?" He twists around so he can see Peyton. "Yeah, she was on his team. That how you got inside with Boone? Pay her off or what?" He turns back to me, sneering now. "Or maybe you put the wood to her and got her to betray—"

I slap him again, hard. This time he stamps his foot on the ground and huffs for a moment like he's having trouble breathing, like a dragon blowing smoke out of its nose. His face has gone the color of rust. "Stop it! Stop it!" he demands.

"I asked you where Josh Boone is."

"I'm trying to tell you," he chokes. "Max Finnerich. It was all him. All his idea. He made the deal with Piotr Malek. *He* brought *me* into all this. I told him no, no way, no chance, but he said he had it all under control. He was in charge of security and security wouldn't be a problem. He was gonna see to it and I knew then what he had in mind, that he was going to kill Matthew, I knew it and I wanted to say something but he threatened my life!"

He punctuates these last three words by punching the air like a boxer on shaky knees trying to hook his opponent but coming up empty. Snot and spittle fly from his mouth as he works himself up and his words shoot out like cannon fire. "Max Finnerich thought he had it all figured out, but he didn't count on two things. He didn't count on Matthew hiring freelance security—*you*—and he certainly didn't think Matthew would change the encryption key and not tell anyone. None of us knew!"

My face is hot. I can feel my cheeks smarting as though he had punched me instead of the air.

Finnerich.

It's all snapping into place and so damn obvious I can't believe I missed it. Finnerich was head of security for Matthew Boone's company before there was a price on Matthew Boone's head. He realized quickly a dead Matthew Boone would be a boon for his enemies and competitors. He just didn't know who would benefit most or how to make contact. So he does his research, either on his own or through Donald Blake, and he lands on Piotr Malek. Malek would hire the assassin, and Finnerich, for a fee, would loosen the defenses, make the hit a cakewalk. That was their deal.

There was a flaw, however. Finnerich didn't expect his boss to reach out to someone like me who might expose his bullshit security. Once Finnerich's half of the bargain went belly-up, he sent his nephews to turn the tables. Except now I don't even believe they *were* his nephews. That bastard's tears and moans and sobs were all a god-damned act. And I let him *walk*. I felt *sorry* for him. I thought he was small time, out of his league, punching above his weight class, but oh, no . . . I was the sucker. He played me like a child's drum.

I knew I was off my game, but I had no idea I was this far off.

I *am* Copeland, not Columbus. I'm not even on the same planet as Columbus.

Blake keeps talking, words peppering me like buckshot.

"So when you showed up and exposed him, he came to me and said we couldn't wait, we had to get Matthew to talk before you got your feet under you. He hired some of his old Blackwater buddies and drew them a map of Boone's place and they were gonna kill you and scare him, but they didn't know you were *so serious*.

"You shot them dead and came right to Finnerich and he thought it was game over, but then you didn't do *anything*. He realized you didn't know, and he thought that while you and the hired killer from L.A. duked it out, he and Carmichael would just kidnap Boone's kid themselves. They went out and bought black masks and they said they had, I guess, *your* cell . . ."

He jerks his thumb at Peyton and her face falls.

She pulls out an iPhone, shaking her head, in disbelief . . . "Finnerich gave me this phone." And it hits her, "Oh, shit." She drops the phone on the ground and crushes it under her boot but little good that does us now.

"Yeah, well, they traced your phone to the woods and they snatched the kid and I was on the horn with their contact in London, Piotr Malek, trying to negotiate the terms, but he was playing hardball, saying he'd already contracted a killer for Matthew Boone and Finnerich said we needed time to get the code, but then we read all about our head of sales dead in a parking lot along with another guy and I told them, no way, fellas, I'm out. I am not into this anymore, do with me what you will, and I got out of there. Just bailed. I could tell Finnerich was pissed, but he's knee deep at this point, and I said, you can negotiate with the Russians yourself, asshole, and just took off and came back here and I guess I was hoping—"

"Where?" I say, my voice sharp.

From my periphery, Archie looks at me funny.

"Where what?"

"Where are they holding the boy?"

"That's what I'm saying . . . I don't know. I told those bastards I was out and they said to hole up and wait for them to call and it all might work out. I think they—"

"They left you alone for us to bite on."

He twists his neck to look back at Archie, then around again to look at me. "What do you mean?"

"Whatever they were gonna do, they're doing it now. Without you. They left you as a big shiny lure but you're a distraction. You're the decoy. It's why you don't have protection, why they didn't shuttle you out of town. They knew all roads led to you, so they left you alone to fend for yourself while they're making the real deal without you."

Archie talks to me, ignoring the man between us. "How long you figure?"

"Not long. They also know this detour is temporary and must've calculated they didn't need much time."

Archie nods at the back of Blake's head, and I catch his meaning. I stand and call out to Peyton. "Go with Archie. I'll meet you downstairs."

"What do we do with . . ." but then she gets it too and lets the question die.

Donald Blake's mind races.

His mouth catches up to his thoughts . . . "No, don't go. Fellas. Lady. I have information. Finnerich needs me. They can't sell it without me. I know the . . ." Peyton files out of the door, and Archie closes it behind them. I take the dishrag out of Blake's hand, and he flinches.

"I can take you to them!"

"You said you didn't know where they are."

I can see on his face he doesn't.

He stammers, "I can get to them. They'll listen to me. I'll get you inside. I—"

His eyes move to my hands.

I'm wrapping my Glock in the dishtowel.

11

Finnerich, Carmichael, Josh.

Is he alive? It's a crapshoot, fifty-fifty odds, maybe less. They snatched him but everything has gone to hell since then, and they may have dumped him and are already on the run. Unless . . .

Unless they didn't need Piotr Malek anymore.

Unless they didn't need Donald Blake anymore.

Unless they cut out the middleman and are dealing directly with the buyers, the Russians.

It hits me. Matthew Boone agreed to it. He gave them the codes. It's why he looked at peace. Why he said he could be alone. Why he took the keys to Archie's Range Rover.

I slam the accelerator and the sedan explodes up the ramp of Interstate 5. I blitz into traffic and start weaving around slower cars, the speedometer climbing.

"What're you doing?" Archie grumbles. His hands find the ceiling as he tries to hold himself in position.

"Boone."

"What about him?"

Peyton looks equally concerned in the rearview mirror.

"He's in contact with Finnerich."

"What're you talking about?"

I barrel the Ford around a minivan, then split the white dotted line as I roar around a tow truck and cross two lanes to the outside, my foot still married to the floorboard.

"He thinks he has a better chance of getting Josh back on his own, making a deal with them. He wanted us to go after Donald Blake, he encouraged us to go, he practically begged us to go."

Archie's face slackens. "Goddamn."

"This exit!" Peyton yells, and I nearly tear the wheel off twisting it down to my lap. The Ford responds, rocketing at an eighty-degree angle to cut across two lanes of traffic and hit the exit without breaking speed.

"Sorry," I manage as the SUV bucks and shudders like a rocket during reentry, but I don't mean it. I'm not sorry.

"Get him," Peyton says for encouragement, touching my shoulder.

—⦚—

The car rips around the bend that leads to the cabin and all three of us see Archie's Range Rover fly by in the opposite direction. Peyton screams "That was him, that was him!" and I react instantly, stomping the brake while keeping my foot on the gas and whipping the wheel to the left, and the SUV spins like a Frisbee. I let the wheel go to stop the tires from turning and the car skids out of its slide, a half-moon of rubber left on the road like a vapor trail, and then we are chasing down the Range Rover from behind like a jungle cat after an elephant.

He might have size, but not much. And I know how to drive.

I tuck in behind him and he swerves erratically to keep me from passing, but he's an amateur and when he overcorrects, I zip up his left side so Archie is looking directing into the driver's window.

Archie hollers, "Pull over!" but Boone ignores him and Archie turns to me and says, "He's got that look."

In the window over his shoulder, the Range Rover closes, fills up the glass like a movie close-up, and gives me a bump. I careen toward the side of the road and brake so he'll come off me and he probably thinks he won, it was that easy, but this time I swoop around behind him and pull up on the opposite side so my window is even with his rear tire.

Peyton gets the same idea as me, rolls down her window, and in sync, we fire, unloading half a clip into that tire; it blows and shreds like a cored apple and the Range Rover fishtails and nearly rolls but somehow keeps its feet on the asphalt before sliding to a stop in the grass that lines the road.

I brake behind it and hurry out from behind the wheel at the same time as Boone jumps down from the wounded Range Rover, enraged, and we meet on the shoulder; he grabs my shirt and tries to yank me off my feet, a man who has probably never been in a fight where there wasn't a seesaw nearby. I plant my feet and he screams, "I have to go! I have to! You have to let me go!"

Archie and Peyton approach on either side of me and wrestle his hands away from where they've bunched up my shirt.

"No, no, no! I have to!"

Archie cuts him off. "Stop, stop."

"No!" he bellows, twisting away from them, but Archie keeps Boone's arms pinned.

"You want your son back?"

"What do you think I'm doing?"

"Killing him! That's what you doing. You gonna get him killed."

Boone turns his spotlight stare on Archie. I step in next to him. "He's right. You think you're doing a good thing because you're tired of feeling helpless and I understand that. Believe me, I do. But if you give Finnerich and Carmichael what they want, then your utility goes away. They get the codes and they cut loose and you'll never see them again."

"We have a *deal*!"

"Donald Blake thought he had a deal."

"Where is he?"

"He doesn't have a deal."

"This is . . . this is . . ."

A car, an old Buick, pulls up. A middle-aged bald man squints at us. "Everything all right?"

Peyton flashes him a smile, holds up her phone like she's on the horn with AAA. "Fender bender. Calling for a tow truck."

The Good Samaritan smiles, placated. "Need a ride?"

"No, we're gonna wait here, but thanks so much for asking. That is *so* sweet."

He grins at her, self-satisfied, and drives off, disappearing over the next rise.

I get into Boone's face so he sees how serious I am. "Can we discuss this somewhere besides the side of the road?"

He looks lost, deserted, grave.

"Come on, Mr. Boone. Leave the Range Rover. Come with us," Peyton coaxes.

"But they're expecting me," he whines.

"Whatever plans you made aren't going to be in your favor. We're going to change that so *we're* in charge, now that we know what they want."

Finally, Boone calms, shrinks. "You think he's alive? You think Josh is alive?"

"I do," I lie.

He believes it. Maybe it's true.

"Let's go now. Let's get out of here," Archie commands, and this time Boone allows himself to be led to Peyton's SUV.

—⁓—

Liam opens the door to the cabin, anxious. His face drops when he sees we don't have his brother with us.

"Liam," his dad says in something that sounds like an apology, but Liam turns and rushes for the stairs, then shoots up to the second floor like a barn bird heading for the rafters.

"I told him I was going to get his brother."

"How did they reach out to you?"

"The drop phone he gave me." He nods my way. "I used it when I called in to talk to Louis Newman, remember? His secretary must've written down the number. I got a call from Donald Blake's phone, only it wasn't Donald. It was Max Finnerich. He said he knew I was with you and he needed me to ditch you and act alone. He said if I did he would give me Josh back. He said to give him the fifty-six-character encryption code today.

"He had Josh call out but I don't know if it was him. I don't know. He sounded muffled, like he was talking through a door. Or maybe his mouth was gagged. I don't know. I think it was my boy. It had to be him. Max came back on the line and told me to meet him at Tick Tock

Storage while you guys were busy with Donald Blake. By now, he knows I'm not coming and he's . . . if you . . . if you . . . kept me . . . if my boy is killed, this is on *you*."

I take a step toward him and Archie gives me his headshake again, no.

I try to speak to him calmly but have a hard time keeping the edge out of my voice. "You were walking into an ambush, Matthew. Trust me, I've seen it, and the end is not pretty. Once they have the information, they can't have Josh around, they can't have you around. They'll go scorched earth. They wanted you to meet at a low-rent storage facility which will be empty, with no security cameras, no witnesses, and they were going to finish it there, get what they needed, and get the hell out of town."

Boone's eyes search the ceiling, seeing nothing, feeling everything. Finally, he exhales, whipped.

"I'm gonna go check on Liam."

"Give me the phone."

He surrenders it absently, then ranges upstairs.

Peyton moves to a small liquor cabinet.

"Anyone else want a drink? I never bartended, but I've sat on a lot of bar stools."

Archie raises a finger.

—⁊⁊—

We stand over a map of Portland and the surrounding area I found in the glove box of Peyton's Ford.

"I bet the paper map business is just about done," Archie muses, and sips a soda and whiskey.

I grimace at him, and he raises his eyebrows.

"What?"

"You wanna focus?"

"I wanna get ripped. This woman can pour a drink."

"There's a pretty good stash here," Peyton pipes up from the kitchen, and appears with some ham and cheese sandwiches. My stomach rumbles. I realize it has been a day since I ate.

"Dig in," she says, and we do.

Between bites, "The detectives who caught this when it jumped off at the park have to be bringing in reinforcements right now, so we gotta be on high alert. I'm sure they've discovered Donald Blake at his apartment in that hotel, and they're upping the manpower, trying to figure out how it's all connected. People saw us at the Yamhill . . . they may not have our faces, but they'll have our sizes, our number, our skin color.

"Yeah, I got a lot of ways around a lot of things, but if the cops jump on us, might be hard to shake and bake. Might be doing a lot of sitting for a long time."

"You want me to check in with some of my old patrol? I got a friend who made detective last year. He could call up to the Portland PD and say he's got something similar down in L.A. and ask what they have?"

I shake my head. "Best to keep our heads down."

"Say no more."

The drop phone buzzes on the table, but I silence it. I imagine Finnerich on the other end, furious, frustrated, slamming his phone down when it gets put to voice mail. I hope it doesn't provoke him into taking it out on Josh if he's alive, but I need Finnerich unhinged and unhappy.

"Wherever we agree upon, we have to get him to here." I point to a spot on the map just south of downtown where a country lane dead-ends into the river. "No way they're bringing him along no matter what they say, so the only important thing is we get an address where they're holding him."

"How?" Peyton asks.

"From what I've gathered, Finnerich thinks he's the smart one and Carmichael's the dummy."

"That's accurate, except Carmichael's one level below dummy. Dummy's here and Carmichael's here." She indicates with her hands.

"Then we need to deal with Carmichael. Good rule of thumb in this line of work: You always want to deal with the dumb-dumb."

"What if someone asks to deal with you, Columbus?" Archie smiles, flares a match, and burns the tip of his cigarette. "That mean you're the dumb-dumb?"

Peyton laughs and it's a good sound. I remember how much I miss that sound, a woman's laugh. I haven't heard it in a long time.

"It's Copeland."

"Uh-uh. Not anymore," he says. "You Columbus."

"Keep it up," I say to Archie, but there's no malice in it, and his grin grows wider.

"There he is again," he says. "Little by little."

—⚉—

I rummage through the cabinets, looking for something sweet, and find a bag of Snickers minis.

"Can I have one?"

I turn to find the older brother, Liam. He looks like an animal that spies a trap and senses there's danger but still wants the bait. His eyes are sunken, brown specks at the bottom of a well.

I crack a hole into the outer bag and hand it to him. I expect him to grab a piece and flee, but he takes a couple of minis and hands me back the bag.

"At my school we have team projects."

We unwrap our candy and pop small pieces in our mouths. I know he wants to talk so I let him.

"It's where a teacher assigns these teams, like at random. Liam, you're four. Mila, you're three. Zoe, you're two. Ramsey, you're one. Like that. Then the fours get together and the threes get together, you get it."

Is Pooley . . . is my son out there right now getting sorted into a group? Is he in kindergarten now? First grade? Is he back in Colorado, or did Jake return to her family in New Hampshire? Does he love her now? Does he remember his mom, his dad, or is it all a dream, like it happened to someone else?

"Our teacher, Mrs. Wagner, always says that it's important we do our part, like if I'm good at writing and maybe Mila is good at drawing, then I do the paragraphs and Mila does the art and maybe Ramsey is a good speaker so he does the presentation, like that. But then she also says if someone's maybe *not* good at anything, or like not, you know, *best* at something, then you should always ask, 'Where can I help?' I've been sitting here, scared, scared to death, while the adults have adult conversations and don't include me and don't think I know what's going on, but I know. I'm not a baby and I'm not stupid.

"My dad thinks Josh is alive and thinks maybe he can get him back. You think he's dead and that doesn't bother you because it'll just help you kill the man who took him. The other two, Peyton and Archie, they're somewhere in the middle. They want to believe he's okay but they look to you as the team leader. So I don't know if he's alive or not, but I'm not ready to give up."

His lips tremble and his eyes shine but he keeps his tears in check, sucking an intake of air like he's trying to catch his breath and then blowing up into his eyes to dry them.

"So I'm going to ask you, Mr. Copeland. How can I help?"

Is this how Pooley will look some day? Brave and earnest and defiant? I think he might.

I lower myself to the floor with my back to the kitchen cabinet so I'm looking up at him. Liam has earned it.

"Here's what you can do. If your brother is alive, and I'm not saying he is, but if your brother is alive, then he's going to need you to help him get over this. He's going to need you to tell him he's strong and he's brave and he's a fighter and that you never gave up. And the reason you never gave up is because you believed *he* would never give up. And you hold him when he wants to be held. And you sleep next to him when the nightmares are overwhelming. And you tell him he's your hero, even though he's your little brother, even when he cries. Can you do that?"

Liam nods. "But I want to help you when you go after Mr. Finnerich."

"I know you do, but the assignment I'm giving you, it's more important than what I'm doing. It's more important than anything I've ever done, and I've lived a lot longer than you, so I know what I'm talking about. I do things to people that messes them up, messes their families up, their friends up, for a long, long time. But what you're going to do for your brother when he gets back? That's giving him life, and only the *best* people, only the *best* brothers, give that."

He stares at me for a long time to see if I'm shining him on, but realizes I'm not. He drops next to me so we're side by side on the floor, unwraps another piece of candy, and pops it in his mouth.

"I can do that," he says.

—⁂—

The phone buzzes again and this time I answer.

"You're dealing with me now," I say with no emotion.

There's a long pause, and for a moment I think the line's gone dead, but Finnerich's voice breaks the silence.

"Put Matthew Boone on."

"I just said, *Max*, you're dealing with me now."

Another long pause, followed by, "I'll kill him. I swear to you."

"Let's meet and talk about that."

"I told Matthew where to meet and he didn't show. There are going to be consequences for that."

"Yeah, well, luckily for Matthew, I kept him from walking into an ambush."

"His boy's blood is on *your* hands."

"Jesus, you sound like what you are, Max. A goddamn amateur."

"I don't—"

"Listen to me because I'm going to talk to you the way professionals do. I have the fifty-six-character encryption code. I don't give a fuck about it. You can jerk off to it in Moscow for all I care. Bring Josh in one hour to the address I text you. From what you know about me, I have no use for police. I'll give you the encryption code and you give me Josh and that'll be the last time we see each other. You don't have to worry about loose ends because we aren't telling anyone anything on our end. We can't and won't, and you know why."

"We meet at the original spot, the Tick Tock—"

"Max, you dumb fuck, we're not negotiating. This isn't give and take. You're not in charge. The only thing you get out of this is the codes. I assume you made contact with the Russian buyer directly, which is why you took your sweet time getting back to us. Good. Great for you. Get your codes, give us the boy, and fuck off."

"Don't you tell—"

I hang up and text him the address, then ignore the phone when it buzzes again. I text him "one hour" and turn off the phone for good.

—⁓—

"Remember when I told you I'm going to need you to access that other side of you? The one who opened that door in the county jail in Los Angeles?"

Peyton sits in the passenger seat of her Ford while I'm behind the wheel. I like this SUV. We've gotten to know each other and the old girl has character. She's grown on me, like her owner.

"I remember."

"This is that time."

"Max Finnerich shot me twice in the chest from behind a mask," she says. "I'm already there."

I rub my chin. It has been weeks since I shaved.

"And when this is done, you think you can go back to a normal life? Turn it off, turn it on?"

"Do you?"

"Nope."

She looks out the windshield, squints her eyes, thinking. "No, I don't think so either."

The clock on the dash reads five to five.

I crank the engine and roll the Ford past a collection of warehouses, past some kind of cannery, and then pull onto a dirt road that may have led to boat access on the Willamette River, but no longer leads anywhere. A couple of orange, faded DO NOT ENTER signs are posted at the end of the road but ivy has reclaimed the area and tugs at the signs, threatening to drag them to the ground. I reach the end of the road and execute a three-point turn so I can face Finnerich when he comes.

I expect he'll be alone, but maybe we'll get lucky.

"Okay," I say, kill the engine, and open my door.

Peyton follows my lead and climbs out of the passenger's side. We move to the front bumper and lean back against the hood. She draws the Strike One knockoff Curtis sold her, keeps it pointed at the ground in front of her, covering the bulk of it with her free hand, like it's natural, casual. I keep my hands free but I'm not going to begrudge her if she wants to get used to the feel of her weapon.

Ten minutes pass before we hear the hum of an engine. The rumble grows louder as a vehicle approaches, and the rubber tires crunch and pop and spit up the gravel road around the corner. Finally, a Jeep Renegade appears and idles twenty yards away.

The Oregon sky is clear for the first time since I arrived in the state and a few of the brighter stars venture out to shine early. The sun brushes the horizon and threatens to drop away completely, like it fears what is coming but wants to bear witness.

Finnerich, alone, cuts the motor on the Jeep and steps out of his driver's side. In his left hand, he holds an automatic pistol. In his right, he carries a phone. He looks like he's been snorting something since the last time we saw each other. His eyes are red-rimmed and tempestuous. He's like a weight lifter who has psyched himself up for the big dead lift, 500 pounds rolled onto either side of the bar. Ropy neck veins bulge, and sweat shines on his forehead and cheeks.

He holds the phone up. "My friend has the boy!"

"Your friend, Carmichael?" Peyton asks, and Finnerich seems to notice her for the first time.

"That's right, you bitch. Carmichael. And if he doesn't hear from me in ten minutes, then he's going to dump the body and disappear so you don't see him again. So give me the codes and—"

"Call him," I interrupt.

"What?"

I raise my voice and enunciate slowly. "I don't believe you."

"I don't give a good goddamn what you believe."

"Call Carmichael or no deal. I want to hear his voice. You can stay over there. We won't move."

Finnerich's vein throbs, pulses. I can see it from here.

"Damn it," he says to himself and punches the number into his phone.

I turn to Peyton. "Can you pinpoint a location if you have the caller on the other end of a cell phone?"

"Yeah, I can get my friend to ping it."

Finnerich talks quickly into his cell and then holds it up high again, like he's showing us a shiny, new trophy. "Okay, Carmichael's on speaker. What do you—"

I am not Copeland and I pull my Glock from its holster and I am a killer and I squeeze the trigger and I am Columbus and I am awake and I am angry and the shot rings out and Finnerich's head jerks back and his blood paints his windshield.

He hits the ground like a puppet with cut strings before the echo of the shot dies.

I don't look at Peyton as I hurry over and scoop up the phone and place it to my ear. "Carmichael, listen to me. Finnerich is dead. I'm standing over his body right now."

"I . . ."

"Don't panic, Carmichael. Be the smart one. Be smarter than you've ever been. Is Josh alive?"

A moment that could go either way, a moment that spools out to infinity. His voice comes through tinny and small. "Yes."

"You're not lying to me?"

"No, he's sleeping."

"Okay, listen. You're going to do exactly what I say because it's the only way you don't end up dead at my feet like Finnerich, okay?"

"Yes."

"Okay, don't hang up the phone. Leave it on and place it next to Josh and wherever you've been thinking about running since this all went bad, run there."

"My mother's?"

"Sure. Go to your mother's. Don't ever come back, okay?"

"Yes."

"Don't forget to leave the phone on, Carmichael."

"I won't."

"Okay. You did good. You're smart."

"Thank you."

I lower the phone and toss it to Peyton. She hasn't moved. She's looking at Finnerich, dead in the dirt, blood still pumping from the hole in the back of his head.

"Let's go get, Josh," I say.

Peyton looks up at me.

"Only a place for good and evil," she whispers under her breath.

—⁂—

The trailer is in the last slip in a mostly empty trailer park. I shoulder the door open and Peyton dashes inside and the interior is dank and dusty and the floor bounces with our steps like it might give way at any moment. Peyton has her gun out—an old cop habit I'm sure—and she presses forward and steps through a curtain and I'm behind her and Josh is handcuffed to a bed, filthy and wan and pallid but alive.

Peyton bounds to him in a single step and claws at the handcuffs that bind his wrist. No sign of Carmichael and I have every confidence he is on his way to his mother's house, wherever that may be.

On the dresser, conveniently left for us to find, is the handcuff key. Crank, crank and I have it unfastened, his arm is free, and Peyton scoops Josh up and he fights her but she shushes him and soothes him and his struggles turn to sobs and the sobs turn to heaves, and she looks at me over his shoulder while she strokes his head.

"Let's get out of this dungeon," she growls.

—m—

We drive to the cabin and Liam is the first one out of the house. Josh hobbles out of our backseat and stands on the gravel driveway with shaky legs but that doesn't stop a big brother from tackling his little brother onto the grass and they are rolling and tumbling and hugging and I'm not sure if they're both laughing or crying and it doesn't matter because they're together.

Peyton wipes tears from the corners of her eyes, sees me notice, and smiles, unashamed.

Matthew Boone steps into the doorway, drawn by the commotion, and slowly realizes the source of the noise. His face contorts, cycling through a spectrum of emotion, and then he croaks a soundless "Josh." His lungs refill, and louder, a wonderful sound now, a joyous sound, a sound a father makes when he finds his lost boy, "Josh!" he shouts, and he sprints across the lawn and piles on top of his sons so they are one rolling, teeming, laughing mass.

Archie steps out on the porch, lights a cigarette, looks from the Boone family to me, and shakes his head, that half smile turning up the corner of his mouth.

Whether he is hoping to see Copeland or hoping to see Columbus, I don't know.

EPILOGUE

Age can creep up on a man, slowly working its hooks into a body and pulling it down over time, like a degenerative disease. Age can also attack all at once, ruthlessly and mercilessly, and rip a man apart in a matter of weeks, days, or hours. Ezra Loeb sits on a bench at the end of the Marina Del Rey pier, staring at Pacific Ocean waves as they roll in, crest, and break. He looks like a faded photograph, browning, curled, and distorted.

"I didn't lie to you. I want you to know that. Not that it matters. But I didn't lie to you," he says.

"You also didn't see the truth."

"That the head of security . . . what'd you say his name was?"

"Finnerich."

"That Finnerich made his deal with Piotr Malek before Malek called me? No. I didn't."

"You got me to take care of your problems. Wilson, Watts, and Malek."

"We made a deal. You agreed to it."

"You could've saved me a lot of time if you knew the details of the goddamn job you took on. You sold yourself as the greatest fence in America. You're not even close. You debase the profession."

Ezra Loeb takes off his glasses, lets out a breath, slow and heavy, and sinks more into the bench.

"Have I made an enemy of you?"

"We're not friends."

He wipes his glasses with his shirt, sets them back on his nose. The waves continue their slow roll from the west, an infinite, inexorable churn.

He makes a gesture with his hand, like he's wiping a chalkboard. "I'm quitting. Releasing my stable. I've had my time. I'll disappear now."

"Good decision."

He sits still and doesn't respond for a long time.

Finally, he says, "I know I would've heard of you. You haven't always gone by the name Copeland."

"No. For a long time, for most of my life, no one called me that."

"Then, please, tell me. What did they call you?"

—⁓—

Summer on the island and school is out. Tourists crowd the boardwalks like pigeons around breadcrumbs. They gawk at the window displays, gorge on fudge, take horse-drawn carriage tours of Fort Mackinac and the Grand Hotel.

The spirit around here is the opposite of when I did my time in Michigan. Sunshine and flowers as opposed to gray sky and endless snow. A butterfly out of a chrysalis. The locals look tired but happy, their pockets stuffed with tourism money like bears with food before winter hibernation.

The board in the window frame I replaced holds. I sit on the steps leading to the kitchen door, hot coffee next to me, skimming the *Detroit Free Press* when Meghan approaches.

"You left," she says.

"Work," I answer.

Meghan dislodges a loose bit of pavement in the driveway with her toe. "You back for long?"

"No. Not for long."

"Who's she?" Meghan looks over my shoulder at Peyton, who exits the door and sits down next to me, careful not to capsize my coffee cup.

"Peyton," she says. "You must be Meghan."

Meghan snorts. "You remembered my name?"

"You're memorable."

"You two married or something?"

It's Peyton's turn to snort. "No. We work together. He's my boss. He's showing me the ropes."

"What do you guys do?"

I turn my eyes to the window frame, then back to the awkward girl on the driveway. "Repair things."

"Also demolition," Peyton adds, and smiles at me.

"Ohhhhkay," Meghan says. "I gotta go to the store for my mom. She has stomach problems or something. I have a list. You guys need anything?"

"We're good, Meghan. It was good to see you."

She raises her palm to shield her eyes and squints at me, checking whether or not I was making fun of her.

"Good to see you, too," she offers skeptically.

—⁂—

Mr. Laughlin expects company.

He has light bouncy music playing through speakers in his living room, dining room, and kitchen. He dances a little soft-shoe as he carries a bottle of cheap vodka to a mixing bowl and upends it. He opens a cherry Jell-O packet, whisks in its contents, and pours the concoction into a pair of rubber ice trays. Vodka Jell-O shots, the kids call them. A good way to get drunk without knowing how fast you got there.

He carefully sets the trays in his freezer and looks around, then claps his hands together, assessing the room. Perfect. The doorbell chimes and he looks at his watch and furrows his brow.

A seventeen-year-old girl wearing a tight strapless top and short-shorts stands on the porch. Mr. Laughlin flashes his lupine smile. "You're early, Pippa."

The girl returns his smile, beaming innocently. "You said seven."

"I did?" Mr. Laughlin asks and chuckles. "Oh, yes, maybe I did, come in, come in," he coos.

She takes a timid step inside his home and looks around. "Aren't there more kids coming?"

"Oh, yes, a few of my summer students. You'll like them. Their parents work at the Grand Hotel just from May to August. Have a seat, have a seat." He gestures at the sofa and Pippa complies. Her shorts ride all the way up her thighs and she tugs at the tops of them but they don't pull down any lower.

Mr. Laughlin searches through a cabinet, then turns, holding up a DVD. "Have you seen *The Dreamers*? A Bertolucci masterpiece."

Pippa shakes her head.

"Of course not, *tsk, tsk*," Mr. Laughlin chides. "Your parents probably frown on mature films."

"They don't let me watch HBO by myself."

"This is the problem. I tell my students to expand the width of their knowledge, but how can they do so when their parents are constantly thwarting their ambition?"

Pippa can't think of a response, so just shakes her head.

"Anyway, give me one minute and I will find something for us to munch."

Mr. Laughlin skips toward his kitchen. It's easy, so easy, that skip says. He only has to put a few thoughts in these virgin heads and they practically—

He jerks to a stop when he sees Peyton pointing a gun at his forehead.

"Shhhh," she says, and puts a finger to her lips.

He holds his breath.

I step in behind Mr. Laughlin and whisper in his ear, "Tell the girl she has to go. You're sorry, but you feel sick all of a sudden."

He nods and takes a step back but I block him.

"Tell her from here."

"Pippa?" he calls out. "I . . . uh . . . you have to go. I feel sick all of a sudden."

I can hear her stir on the couch and stand. Her voice sounds concerned. "Oh, okay. Can I—"

"Tell her to just go. Do it now," I whisper.

"Just go, Pippa!"

Moments later, the door opens and closes, and Pippa's footfalls echo off the wooden porch and then recede. The front gate swings open and then slams closed.

Mr. Laughlin cranes his neck to look at me and then at Peyton.

"I don't have much money here."

"We're not here to rob you."

"I don't . . . I don't understand."

"How many girls, Mr. Laughlin?"

"What?"

"How many girls have you assaulted?" Peyton asks as she opens up the freezer and pulls out the ice trays.

"I . . . I . . ." he stutters.

Peyton flings the ice trays at him so the red Jell-O streaks across his face and oozes down his cheeks.

"How many girls have you raped?" she asks, a bite in her voice.

"Oh God," he says, wiping his eyes with the backs of his hands.

"Not even close," Peyton answers.

"I don't know what your daughter told you . . ."

"Wrong again," Peyton says. "We're not parents."

"Then who . . . who are you?"

Peyton looks at me for the answer.

I am Columbus.

The way I live is to have something to live for.